I0746710

Edited by ERIC RAGLIN
Foreword by KATHE KOJA

Cover art copyright © 2021 by Lynne Hansen, LynneHansenArt.com

Edited by Eric Raglin

Interior Design, Typesetting, and Layout by Sam Richard

CONTENTS

EVERYBODY'S MONSTER
BY KATHE KOJA

Antifa, anti-fascists, anti-fascism: we recognize resistance when we see it, when we enact it, on the barricades, at the ballot box and the mailbox, the sidewalk and the keyboard, fighting back and working hard to create a world of plurality, of us, all of us: not perfect, but in process, together.

Are we sure that we can recognize fascism?

Not just the online screeds and rhetoric—and there's so much of it —the sly hand-signals and podium shouts; not just the fascists, zealots and bigots, year after year, who advance and serve that ideology; not just the confused and the ignorant who flirt with it, stupidly fascinated, the way you flirt with a gas can and a match; but the actual thing itself. We see its effects, but can we see an ideology?

Do you know what a tick looks like? Imagine a tick.

Imagine a tick with a human face.

Horror as a genre, and most especially splatterpunk, is unafraid of blood. It's unafraid to get its hands dirty, to look hard, to stare, and pull into focus whatever it finds. This anthology does that service for us unflinchingly, through the varied voices of its talented and dedicated writers: identifies, through circumstance and scenario and era, past changing names and acronyms, that small monster. These stories and their writers all say, Let's get a look at that tick, let's get close, and examine how it clings to its host, how it inches and sucks and bloats; how it gloats. How it always has the same taste for blood: it can be gagging-full, but it's so thirsty. It's always thirsty because it's always arid, it's empty, it can't create, it can only destroy. (That's one of the real tells of evil, I personally believe: all it can make is nothing.)

These stories are fierce, are subtle, are sad, are shocking: and are not at all afraid. Because these writers say with these stories *We see you, tick with the human face, we recognize your face, we know you're there and we know how to call you out.*

Reading these stories is a very healthy exercise in identification, in case you find yourself confronted with that human-faced tick. Because, though these stories may inhabit a reality more extreme than any we may ever meet, we can all do the first best thing: see the monster, everybody's monster. And starve it.

Starve, tick. Starve.

ONE OF THE GOOD ONES, OR: IT'S A GAS!

BY GORDON B. WHITE

A cop walks into a bar. Officer Johnny Royal of the [REDACTED] P.D., to be exact, still in powder blue with after-shift scruff, walks into Grady's Droop.

Busy night at Grady's. Neon signs for domestics glisten hot pink and ozone teal off the short-shorn patrolmen stuffed into the bucket booths. Stubbled detectives wipe nicotine-stained cuffs across the condensation on the copper-top bar. The blown-out jukebox blares and makes mud of the policemen's bawl.

It's hot, too. Deep summer. Inside Grady's, slack-jawed humidity and steaming skin make a swamp. The poor air conditioner out back must be on its last gasp because the gold ribbon streamers tied to the vents wag like sick tongues before falling limp.

"Fucking dead," someone yells.

Johnny stakes an elbow on the bar, badge on his beat-blues blinking like a tin heart's beat. Raises one finger to Drea who's working the taps like slots at the far end. She nods, weary, lip pouched to bogart an invisible smoke.

Drea tops a pint, backhands the head off, slaps it at a sergeant who hangs like a soaked sheet from the corner's brass pole. Sarge coughs up some moist greenbacks and Drea stuffs them into her apron without counting. If you can't trust the police, right?

Back to Johnny, Drea leans in close. Johnny smells her mash of Juicy Fruit and Nicorette. Sees crow's feet cracks beneath her foundation's plaster. When she smiles, her teeth are lipstick bloody.

"Harry said to send you back." She jerks a chipped-polish thumb towards Grady's recesses. Past the pool tables with their skid-marked felt and the hazmat bathroom. Back to where the steel door to the BACK-back looms like a tombstone.

Johnny's about to push-off when Officer Andy Holder from the precinct, now in jeans and sweat-drenched tee, wedges in and pins Johnny to the bar.

"Drea!" Andy yells from six inches away. "AC's fuckin' dead a-fuckin'-gain!"

"Fuck you want me to do?" she yells back.

"Fix it!" Andy hollers. The sweltering crowd hoots in echo: "Fix it! Fix it!"

Drea raises her hands and retreats. She opens the fuse box panel on the wall behind the well bottles.

"What's with you?" Andy slurs as his greasy fingers pluck at Johnny's blue shirt. "Not hot enough for ya?"

Drea flips the breaker. A click like a hammer falling, and then the whole bar shudders as if being defibrillated. Everything dies for half a heartbeat, then roars back as the air conditioner hacks and sputters to life. The golden ribbons on the grates above flutter as the circulatory wheeze resumes. Wiping her hands on her apron like a back-alley surgeon, Drea returns.

"Harry's waiting," she says to Johnny. "Something for the road," she squints at him, "or are you still working?" And just like that, the weight of the attention of the Boys-Not-in-Blue collapses onto Johnny's uniformed shoulders

Why is Officer Johnny Royal here? they're thinking. Why is he dressed like that? Does he think he's one of the good ones?

Johnny also realizes he's twisting his wedding ring in circles like a bolt that will never quite tighten. He thinks of Sam at home. Johnny asks himself the same thing: *Why is he here?*

"Whiskey," he mutters. Holds up two fingers. "Double."

Drea smiles wide enough for a gold canine to gleam. Officer Andy backslaps Johnny hard enough to sting before he melts into the crowded scene in the bar's mirror. Over Johnny's shoulder, the pressed bodies emit a visible fug. The stale air reeks of meat and cordite even as the resurrected air conditioner tries to stir the limp yellow ribbons in its thin stream. Beads of sweat beneath Johnny's starched blue shirt make crescents under his arms like the laughing faces of Comedy Masks. *Why is he here?* Indeed.

The crack of rocks glasses against the copper-top bar snaps Johnny back. Two tumblers filled to sloshing with mud-colored spirits.

Drea winks, sweaty mascara gumming her lids. "Double."

A COP WALKS INTO A BACKROOM. Officer Johnny Royal, to be exact, carrying two glasses of rotgut that dribble down his wrists with every step. The BACK-back room of Grady's Droop, too, which is the dimly lit loading dock of an adjoining business that dried up in the last recession. Rapid Response Officer Harrison "Harry" Crant is leaning on a wooden crate and tucking a pinch of tobacco in his lower lip. A green tarp hangs off the crate like a tablecloth. Another R2—Bushrod Jefferson—is pacing, his big beard frosted blue in his smart phone's glow. Meaty thumbs tap out sausage codes on the glass.

Harry and Bushy are dressed in their civilian rags, which are, if anything, even more combat-ready than their Rapid Response gear. Steel-toe boots with horse teeth treads; pants with more pockets than Grady's lopsided pool tables. Matching trucker caps bearing a bleach-white skull over Rambo knives instead of crossbones mark their membership in the same "social club": the Happy Fellas.

Harry raises a hand to Officer Johnny Royal. "Cousin." The word trickles out with the Kodiak chaw into his stained goatee. "How goes it?" Without waiting for an invitation, he takes one of Johnny's whiskies. Wads the tobacco up inside one cheek, takes a long pull of booze from the other. Sighs; nods; farts.

"That'll do me right," Harry laughs. He smiles but holds it like a weapon.

Johnny knows what the R2s want to see. So, he takes a long drink of whisky, and he coughs, and Harry laughs while Bushy shakes his head, but that display sets them right. Even if Johnny is still dressed like a stickler, he must be one of the good ones.

"So," Johnny says once he catches his breath. "What did you want to show me?"

Harry pushes up off the crate and pulls back the tarp to reveal a yellow logo stenciled across the weathered wood. It's a rough harp shaped like a toothy grin, fluffy wings on the corners like smirking cheeks. In blocky caps: *UNEEDA MUNITIONS SUPPLY. You need it … we got it!*

"Know what this is?" Harry kicks the side with a steel-toe and Bushy flinches at the thunk.

Johnny shakes his head. "Looks old."

"Shit's been banned since 'Nam," Bushy calls over like he was in the shit, although Johnny knows Bushy's barely thirty.

"Real MK Ultra type shit," Harry adds.

Johnny squats for a closer look. Crate's old, maybe even Vietnam old. Also, what Johnny took for a harp and wings is actually a row of cartoon bullets bookended by mushroom clouds. Still shaped like a smile, though.

UNEEDA MUNITIONS. Sounds like a joke.

"Is it safe?" Johnny asks.

As if in answer, Bushy's cellphone buzzes in his hand and he nods to Harry. Harry spits, says, "We're gonna find out."

Bushy heads to the rolling metal bay door and hoists the chain like a theater curtain. Right on cue, a black van with no lights rolls in and cuts the engine. The chain clanks again as Bushy lowers the gate, but Harry raises a hand to stop it short. Maybe a foot of space—enough for an errant breeze, maybe. Enough space that Johnny can hear the asthmatic air pump just outside struggling to keep the cops back in

Grady's Droop from wilting. It still sounds like its death is coming at any moment.

The black van disgorges two more R2s: Ram and Ted. Johnny knows their names, but Rapid Response are [REDACTED] P.D.'s cowboys and he's just the tinhorn who happens to be married to Harry's cousin, Sam. Johnny twists the band around his finger again, but there's no resistance. It just spins as he watches Ram and Ted slip their Happy Fellas caps on and pull up bandannas over their noses and mouths. They throw the van's sliding side door open.

"Any trouble scooping one up?" Harry asks as Ram and Ted drag some kid out of the back.

"Nah," Ram grunts. "Blocks're lousy with them."

"Nobody'll miss this one," Ted adds.

Kid's maybe twenty, tops. Thin with smooth cheeks, pink hair, wearing all black except for the yellow plastic zip ties pinning their hands behind their back. Their fingers are purple, two of them bent wrong. The kid kicks a little, but it's clear most of the fight's been wrung out. Ram cuts the cuffs loose so Ted can slap the kid into a folding chair, then they zip each wrist and ankle to the seat. The four R2s gather around to admire their handiwork before turning back to scope Johnny.

"You sure he's cool?" Ted asks. Tucks his thumb behind the circlet of restraints at his hip like a golden lasso.

"My cousin's frosty," Harry says.

Bushy coughs. "Cousin-in-law."

"We're all in-law here," Harry says and chuckles at his own joke. "Besides, if we aren't in blood right now, we will be soon. Right, my man?"

Johnny just stammers: "I, I don't know what you mean."

Harry winks. "You will." He elbows Bushy, gestures to the crate. "Let's set up."

As they pry the lid off the Uneeda Munitions box, the scene is crystal clear even if the significance is not. Officer Johnny Royal, still holding half a whisky, stands alone. Rookie; in-law; bystander. Audience to the show the Rapid Response Happy Fellas are putting on with the pink-haired kid strapped to a chair in the loading dock behind Grady's Droop where every [REDACTED] cop who isn't swinging a truncheon downtown is getting sloppy.

To Johnny's left, Bushy tosses handfuls of mildewed straw from the Uneeda crate and Harry pulls out a metal canister that's been spray-painted the color of goldenrod. To Johnny's right, Ram and Ted lean on their sobbing hostage. Behind the metal door back inside, the barroom is a murky roar. Out past the half-rolled gate, the ancient AC struggles to do its one job.

Then the pump sputters, hacks. Dies. A low booing reverberates from inside Grady's, then even out here the lights flicker when Drea flips the breakers inside. The AC gasps as it's jerked back into its life of never-ending service, but a muted cheer erupts from behind the door.

Beyond the roll gate, a siren wails in the distance. Crying, maybe, but it could be tears of laughter.

STOP me if you've heard this one before, but a cop walked up to a bar. Well, future cop. Johnny Royal, [REDACTED] P.D. cadet, to be exact, and the bar was City Hall's railing.

He raised his hand. Swore to serve and protect. Officer Johnny Royal's heart swelled three sizes as they pinned on the badge. Might as well have read: Johnny Good Apple.

And Johnny has a family: father, mother, younger brother. A husband, Sam, whose cousin is also a cop—one of the wild bunch in the Rapid Response. But [REDACTED] isn't a backwards place; it's progressive. When Johnny and Sam are out together, the only dirty looks are from people who know Johnny's a cop.

And that burns him, just a bit, if he's just being honest. Because sure, America's police have their problems. And yes, in [REDACT-ED], too. But overall, they're good. They're good to Johnny and Johnny is a good one, too. Most people could see that, it seemed. At least, before this summer.

Because this summer has been hell. Every night downtown [REDACTED] is filled with anarchists in black, throwing brickbats and firecrackers. Hiding behind the other screaming protesters who are breaking curfew, too. Umbrellas, milk jugs, cans of soup; everything is a weapon once you look at it right. Stay on the streets long enough and you'll see all the broken windows.

Still, Officer Johnny Royal of the [REDACTED] PD holds the line, even while his younger brother calls him a pig, as if this were the 70s. While on the TV, half the city calls for his job. They want to ruin him, after all he's done to keep them safe.

The last time Johnny's brother spoke to him was at a family dinner that, charitably speaking, did not end well. "How do you live with yourself?" he asked.

"It's my job," Johnny said.

A bitter laugh from his brother. "If my job required me to gas innocent people, I'd find a new job."

Sam, sitting beside Johnny, squeezed his knee under the table.

What Johnny wanted to say, maybe, was: It's complicated. Or, that the alternative is worse. Or, who was he to question the hard decisions others made to keep the peace?

That it hurts him, too. That in the early dawn he crawls into his husband's arms and he can't even speak, but what else is he supposed to do? It's not just him; it's not just [REDACTED]. It's something so much bigger that he can't even begin to get his arms around it, and it scares the living fuck out of him, but what is there to do but press on?

What Johnny really wants, in his heart of hearts, is to say that he's one of the good ones. If Johnny's doing it, then it isn't *really* bad? And if Johnny quits, then what's left?

Instead, what Officer Johnny Royal of the [REDACTED] P.D. said to his brother was: "If they're out there, they aren't that innocent."

When the outside world is against you, where is there to go but deeper inside? Officer Johnny Royal puts in for a transfer to join cousin-in-law Harry in the Rapid Response.

A COP WALKS into a moral conundrum. Officer Johnny Royal of the [REDACTED] P.D. out back of Grady's Droop watches through a full-face gas mask's fogging goggles as four other cops, all R2s wearing similar masks and Happy Fellas hats, stand around a pink-haired kid zip-tied to a chair.

Cousin Harry lifts a chemical spray fogger by its pistol grip. Looks standard, except instead of pepper spray it's screwed onto an antique yellow canister with the *Uneeda Munitions* stencil of smiling bullets and smirking mushroom clouds. Harry lifts the bottom of his mask, spits a streak of tobacco between the kid's feet, then slips it back down.

"Ready?" he asks.

"Hell yeah," Bushy says.

Ram says, "Yep."

Ted pulls the kid's head up by the pink hair. "Open wide."

Harry pulls the trigger. A brief hiss and sputter, then the *Uneeda* belches up a cloud of mustard yellow steam that swallows the kid. The consistency isn't like any spray or gas Johnny's seen deployed, but the kid screams like normal. They're gasping and choking, spitting and yowling. They thrash against the wrist and ankle restraints, then convulse once and slump in the chair like a puppet with cut strings.

Harry lets up and the yellow fog disperses a bit, although its particulate taint still halos the group.

"Holy shit," Johnny says. "Is ... Did you?"

"Watch," Harry hisses from inside his mask.

With a snap, the kid's head jerks up, a flamingo swash of matted hair. They snarl, split lips curled like a cornered dog's as strands of frothing spittle stream from bloody teeth. Eyes, though? Not red like Johnny would expect from tear gas or pepper spray. Instead, the whites are filmed with a cloudy yellow haze.

With a howl the kid throws themself against the restraints and the chair's joints groans.

"Holy fuck!" Bushy laughs and literally jumps with glee. "That shit works!"

Ram and Ted nod at each other in approval.

"I told you." Harry raises his mask completely up over his head and spits again, this time right in the kid's chest. The kid is too consumed by growling and yanking at their restraints to notice.

Johnny stutters behind his mask. "Wha— wha—?"

"What this is," Harry says, "is an end to this summer of violence." He squats down like a ranch hand to look at the kid, but all that's left in those eyes is a roaring golden anger. Harry laughs. "Fucking peaceful protests, my ass. One whiff of this, they'll tear each other to pieces."

Bushy, Ram, and Ted all lift their masks, too. Clearly, they no longer care about witnesses.

"This is wrong," Johnny says. The words just kind of fall from him, but they make enough sound as they hit the floor that Bushy turns around.

"What was that?" he asks. "Fucking hell, Harry. I told you this goddam f—"

"Hey!" Harry snaps Bushy off. Jabs a finger in the other R2's chest. "You watch your fucking mouth. You use that kinda language, and you and me, we're gonna have some problems."

Bushy blushes, chagrinned, but Ram speaks up from behind the kid, still snarling in the chair. "Man's got a point, Har. He's not one of us."

"Yet," Harry says.

"Maybe," Bushy says, still sulking.

Ted grunts in agreement. Suddenly, everyone around Johnny looks fit to take a bite of him.

This is the time to say something, Johnny knows. Take the high road; take a stand; take his lumps if necessary. He didn't sign up for *this*. Officer Johnny Royal walks into an ethics problem, sure, but knows what he should say.

What Officer Johnny Royal does say, though, is: "I mean, don't you think riling them up like that is dangerous? Look at the freak." The other cops smirk: they like that word even as the echo haunts the gas mask still hiding Johnny's face. He tries again: "Aren't they just as likely to hurt us as each other?"

"Nah," says Harry. "This stuff should only last a few minutes.

That's half of what we're testing here." The other Happy Fella R2s chuckle in unison.

"Besides," Bushy chimes in, "we're much better at doing the hurting."

Harry laughs. "That's the other half."

On cue, Ram punches the kid hard enough to rock the chair and half a tooth skitters across the floor. The kid doesn't notice, though. Not yet.

Then Harry, Bushy, Ram, and Ted kettle the kid, swinging and slamming fists into their face. Bushy stomp kicks them, and the chair topples, the kid's head making a cartoonish coconut clonk as it hits the ground. Doesn't faze the kid, though, because they're still flopping like a fresh fish nailed to a plank.

The scrum circles the kid. Johnny hears steel toes on bones with not enough meat; the folding chair's screech as it slides across the concrete; the muted swish when blood lubricates it. Beneath it all, the kid's furious howl lasts far too long until Harry gives one final field kick like Charlie Brown getting the football, and the kid's sounds shatter.

Harry, Bushy, Ram, and Ted step back, panting. Other than their heavy breathing and the arthritic air conditioner still pumping away just beyond the roll gate, the only other sound is the blood in Johnny's ears.

The R2s rest their arms in sevens at their sides and look down. Kid's gotta be dead, Johnny thinks. He just witnessed a murder.

So much for being one of the good ones.

Then a cough and a sputter from the ground. A low moan. The kid's not dead after all.

It isn't too late for Officer Johnny Royal.

Harry shakes his head, scattering sweat beads. "Holy shit."

"We need to call an ambulance," Johnny says. It's soft, though, muffled by the mask he hasn't yet been able to remove. The others don't respond.

"We need to call an ambulance!" Johnny yells it this time, his voice blown out behind the vents.

Harry hears that. Slowly turns.

"Nah, cousin. We're not doing that." Harry picks up the gas sprayer by the handle and shakes it to hear the magic dust still sloshing in the rusty yellow canister. "But that does remind me," he says. "What do you call a drunk cop that kills someone?"

Johnny, uncomprehending, chokes: "What?"

"A cab!" Harry howls out the punchline.

The R2s cackle, ragged and frenzied in the adrenal afterglow. Bare cheeks ruddy with the flush of blood; eyes wild. Johnny feels their hunger.

Harry's smile withers. Six feet away, he points the gas canister at Johnny. "Round Two, cousin. You want to be part of the family, give it a squeeze."

Johnny shakes his head, his gas mask's nozzle flopping like a trunk.

"Think of it as science," Harry says. "We need to see what a second dose'll do."

Bushy has walked over and picks up the prybar resting against the Uneeda Munitions crate. Ram cracks his knuckles. Ted just frowns.

"You're going to do it," Harry says. He doesn't even add "or else."

The kid on the floor is whimpering, but each breath is drawing out longer towards a sob. The Uneeda gas having run its course, the pain is setting back in. Who knows what another blast will do? What license it might give to the R2s?

Johnny knows this is it: that he's standing on the cusp of that *something so much bigger*. That *something* so massive that even staring directly at it he still can't quite make out the contours or the shape. He wants to say, just give me a minute. Just let me think.

"Now," Harry shouts and throws the gas sprayer to Officer Johnny Royal.

Johnny catches it out of the air and the gravity sends a shockwave through his arms. A flash of clarity and surge of virtuous anger fill him.

"No," Johnny says. And he throws the sprayer to the ground with righteous purpose.

But the instant it leaves his hand, Johnny realizes his mistake. The whole apparatus falls apart in slow motion. The yellow metal canister is reflected in the R2s' unmasked eyes as it makes a cartoon clang on the concrete. The aged aluminum ruptures right where it connects to the sprayer handle, spewing smoke like a sulfur volcano as it pinwheels across the floor.

YOU KNOW THE DRILL. Cop walks into a gas cloud. Officer Johnny Royal in the saffron-pollen gloom, hindered further by the fogged lenses of a gas mask that only he was still wearing when the canister burst. There's just screaming, everywhere.

Down by the van, the bulk of Ram and Ted slam again and again into metal and glass. In one lurch, Ram's head emerges from the haze, eyes yellow cataracts and lips deranged into a snarl, deep fingernail furrows across his scalp like pizza slices. Then Ted's ham of a hand follows from the fog, grips an ear and tears it halfway off as he pulls Ram back in.

The gate, Johnny thinks. If he can roll it open, let the poison air out, it should only take a minute or two to calm down. He can still salvage something. He takes a step towards the gate.

Wood splinters behind him as Harry and Bushy slam each other against stacks of crates. Johnny turns to see precarious boxes teeter as Harry is ripping big handfuls of Bushy's beard out by the bloody roots. Bushy sinks a thumb into Harry's eye socket and Johnny feels the pop as he watches. They claw at each other as they careen into the *Uneeda* crate. Under the press, the rotten wood gives and another dozen antique cylinders clatter out over one another like rusty stinkbugs onto the concrete. Hissing with laughter, they giddily spray their poison into the air and the enormous billow swallows everything.

Arms waving, Johnny turns back to swim through the soup. In the thickening fog, he hears bones crunching and flesh tearing. The howling shadows grappling with each other might as well be moun-tains in the distance until Johnny's grasping right hand brushes someone's arm. Either Ram or Ted—even Harry or Bushy, maybe, if they've gotten this far—grabs Johnny's wrist.

Then pain.

Just a fuck-ton of pain, as something moist crunches down on Johnny's right middle and index fingers. Blinded by smoke, Johnny feels them gnawing, sucking on his fingers. Biting. Chewing. He's about to vomit into his mask from the pain when another dark shape crashes into the first. The impact tears Johnny's wrist from the other's grip and Johnny's fingers from his hand. The sensation of air on new flaps of skin at the stubs is a wretched novelty.

Behind the yellow curtain, someone squeals as something wet is loudly torn from a place where it shouldn't leave and a dark wave licks at Johnny's shoes. Sobbing into his mask, he crushes his mangled hand up under his sweaty armpit and presses on, because what the hell else is he going to do?

He stops. This isn't right.

After being spun around in the dandelion haze, which way is he going? The roar and whorl of violence around him is too much. He can't make heads or tails of—

With a rasp and groan, the decrepit air conditioner pump outside coughs itself into a shuddering demise yet again. That croaking rupture, though, is enough to give Johnny a rough heading. He heads towards it.

Then, there! A meagre light ahead where the smoke seeps out beneath the roll gate. The ancient pump just beyond is silent, but Johnny is almost to the gate. Just five more feet.

Johnny stumbles. His ankle rolls, drops him to a knee. Practically blind behind the mask, he gropes with his good hand to find the obstruction.

Metal. A tube. Connected to another.

Oh.

What's left of a metal folding chair.

He lifts the broken leg to confirm. Squints at the glove hanging from a yellow plastic loop. Rubber? Nitrile? He touches it with one of his remaining fingers. Warm and wet.

Oh.

Then there's the kid, beat to hell but standing. Pink hair soaked red. Right between Johnny and the chain to raise the gate. The raw muscles of the kid's naked hand glisten in the wedge of light.

With what's left of his own hand, Officer Johnny Royal finally draws his gun.

A COP WALKS INTO A BAR. Officer Johnny Royal of the [REDACTED] P.D., to be exact, staggers back into the main room of Grady's Droop. Still wearing a gas mask, covered in enough blood to make his beat-blues bruise purple. Two fingers bit to stubs, each heartbeat sends little crimson squirts around the grip of his empty service nine-mil.

Johnny staggers in and every eye turns to him. He drops the empty pistol. Rips the mask off and gulps for air.

"Call," he coughs out, "call the…" But it dies on his tongue.

Dead silence. No one is speaking. No music is playing. Not even the air conditioner is running. Everyone is staring at him. They must have heard the screams. The shots.

Then there's a click like a hammer falling as Drea flips the breaker. The whole bar shudders, then the air conditioner breaks the silence with a jolly wheezing laugh. With a snap, the yellow ribbons on the grates flutter in proud salute as the first plumes of Uneeda Munitions' goldenrod smoke spill out into the bar.

Officer Johnny Royal begins to laugh. This is a joke; it has to be.

One of the good ones.

THE BOOK OF VEILS
BY KEITH ROSSON

Chris Shaw had been a member of the Aryan Patriots before forming his own splinter group, Our White Nation, after endlessly butting heads with leadership of AP. They were, in his mind, not nearly committed enough—violently or otherwise—to forging an ethnostate for white, patriotic Americans, one whose borders and precepts would be strictly enforced. OWN was, in his own words, "a fucking hardcore unit," and as he manned his booth in the cavernous building that held the weekly Southside Flea Market, he ran through a mental checklist of necessary equipment and tasks he and the other OWN members would need to get done for next weekend's White Freedom March through downtown Portland. Now that he was done with the Aryan Patriots and running his own outfit, his crew looked to him for guidance. There were multiple guys from out-of-town white power orgs coming in as well, and they'd need accommodations. Lot of moving parts to ensure that the basement-dwelling socialists of antifa got their faces stomped in in a week's time.

Chris owned a contracting outfit, working with a network of plumbers, electricians, and carpenters. He hired his friends and was well known in Neo-Nazi and white supremacist circles as a guy who could line you up some work. He prided himself on it. He also ran a booth at the flea market once a month, selling various antiques and collectibles, most notably from the Civil War and World War II eras. Lot of Confederate flags, German Lugers, Panzer helmets and swastika medallions. Armbands, bayonets, shit like that. Chris was unapologetic and unrepentant about his inventory and full of dark mirth whenever someone walked up to his booth to give him shit. The owners and organizers of the market, Jim and Linda, had fielded every complaint imaginable over the six years Chris had tabled there, and he took great comfort in the fact that they had his back. Linda had long since taken the "I'm not a fan, but I believe in the First Amendment" route, while Jim had bought a Stasi officer's hat from him, and a hardcover edition of *Mein Kampf.* Fuck all the doubters and subhuman sympathizers was Chris's staunch belief, including this fool who was walking up to him now with a look like he'd just bitten into dogshit and didn't know whether to spit or swallow.

Chris stood up at the man's approach, his arms folded, his chin lifted. He still swung a hammer often enough to appear formidable, and the ink covering him from neck to hands did a lot to dispel any potential fuckery. The gentlemen standing before him didn't pause, though, just came right up with that sour look on his face as he cast a glance about Chris's table.

"Can I help you," Chris said, sounding like he'd prefer to do anything but.

"Hopefully," said the man, squinting down at a collection of tintypes on the folding card table heavy with Chris's wares. He picked one up: various war dead, Northern boys in some field outside of Vicksburg, the bodies littering the photo like ghosts, pale and shimmery things in the grass. "I'm looking for a very particular book."

The guy was maybe in his fifties. Cadaverously pale. Glasses that needed cleaning, thinned, corkscrewed hair. He looked, in his buttonup and slacks, like an academic who had been awakened suddenly from a deep sleep. Chris Shaw trusted his instincts, and his dislike of this man was immediate and grating.

"We handle collectibles, mostly. Not a lot of books here."

The man adjusted his glasses and peered at Chris through the lenses, his eyes owlish and distorted. *"The Book of Veils* is the title I'm interested in."

Chris smiled. "Ah, I see. And you think I would have a book like that."

"Well," said the man, lifting his chin at the framed poster of Heinrich Himmler that hung on the wall behind Chris.

"Yeah, no," Chris said. "Sorry."

"Even a later printing. Even a reproduction," the man said. "A pirated copy, as it were."

"I deal in antiques. Not novelty items."

"Is that what you consider it?"

"I do."

"Your compensation would be generous."

"Look. How many times can I tell you no," Chris said, leaning forward and tenting his fingers on the table, "before I have to go around there and convince you?"

The man got the point. With a curt nod, he walked away. Didn't check any other booths out. Just walked right out the door.

THE NEXT DAY AT WORK, Chris couldn't stop thinking about it. The man and his tucked-in shirt, his trousers with the crease. Looking like he'd stepped out of a classroom thirty years ago. Asking for a book, *that* book. Chris trafficked in incendiary shit—he'd sold a Klan hood last year and news stations had interviewed him, Linda, and Jim all about it, made it into a big fucking thing—but it was all factual, historical, *reputable* stuff. *The Book of Veils* ... that wasn't. That was some horror movie, cosplaying bullshit. The only copy he'd ever heard of was in Mel Tucker's collection, and even Mel said the thing was bad news. Mel, with his four tears tattooed beneath his eye, his stretch at Pelican Bay. *88* tattooed on his throat, each number of the size of a fist.

The day started out poorly—he got a call from a client out in Milwaukee with a complaint. So he called Mitch on his cell phone, had him meet Chris out at a house he was doing a bid on. Mitch met him at noon, walked up to where Chris was surveying this house where a couple wanted an add-on done. The couple wasn't home and Chris just laid into him right there in the backyard with the birds chirping and everything.

"What the fuck, man. This client calls me and tells me you're up there yesterday putting flashing on her roof with your fucking shirt off."

Mitch just looked at the ground.

Chris got close, close enough that Mitch had to look up. "You had your tats showing," Chris said. "Right? This nice lady's got some miscreant up on her roof with his swastikas hanging out. Iron Crosses and 88s and shit, for all the neighbors to see."

Mitch said, "Dude, it was like ninety degrees out yesterday."

"I don't give a shit. You wear a shirt on my jobs, you feel me?"

"Cool."

"Cool what?" Chris said.

Mitch looked away. "Cool, boss, I'll wear a shirt."

Chris nodded. "Good." And because a good leader always allowed his warriors to save face, Chris gripped him around the back of the neck and grinned. "You ready to stomp some antifa skulls this week-end, baby? See how well a bunch of socialists can crowdfund their hospital bills?"

"I'm ready," said Mitch, still stung.

"I'm gonna need you, man. You're my attack dog."

Mitch said it was cool, but he walked back to his truck without looking back, and Chris couldn't shake that uneasy feeling.

The Book of Veils, it snagged at him like a bad dream.

THAT EVENING, Chris met up with his crew at the Slag Hole, a Southeast bar sympathetic to their views. He got there early and ate a cheeseburger while going through his various burner accounts on social media, stirring shit. His online personas were relentlessly fascist and violent, and he took great joy from getting blocked by the little "anarchist" leftists. He was feeling better by the time guys started rolling in.

Chris Shaw *loved* Portland protests. Fucking loved them. It was no secret that law enforcement was on their side; just look who they arrested and gassed and who they didn't. More than once riot cops had been filmed making the white power "OK" hand gesture at their rallies, and Chris and other far-right organizers were always contacted by the cops before rallies to coordinate movements and police placements. Nine times out of ten, groups like OWN and Aryan Patriots were given free rein to instigate melees with the leftists, provided they kept it to a cordoned off area. Then the cops arrested the commies, cracking heads and macing them, while Chris and his ilk were usually afforded police escorts back to their rented busses on the edge of downtown.

It was gladiator shit, and not only permitted by the city and its law enforcement but tacitly encouraged. Chris slavered over it. Fucking with antifa gave him purpose. At the bar, he and his crew downed IPAs and fantasized openly about killing antifa members, getting loud about it. They painstakingly pored over footage from previous protests, marveled over landed punches or baton strikes, or where mace had doubled someone over. Chris was pretty sure he'd broken a woman's jaw at the last protest in Salem, this little black bloc chick with tattoos on her neck, and months later it had taken on a nearly sexualized cadence in his mind.

He stepped out into the parking lot of the Slag more than a little buzzed. A hot wind blew through the lot, stirring up the scent of warmed asphalt. Everyone called out to each other as they got in their rigs, catcalls and bullshit, and Chris felt good; they were prepped for this weekend. He was already on the road, wind ripping through the cab of the truck, when his cell rang. He didn't recognize the number.

He turned the stereo down. "Yeah."

"Mr. Shaw, this is Edmund Pelletier. We spoke yesterday."

One word from the man's mouth and he recognized the voice. The prissiness. "How'd you get this number?"

"Well, you're not a hard man to find. Christopher Shaw, Shaw Contracting and Construction? I Googled you."

"What do you want, Edmund?"

"I feel like we got off on the wrong foot."

"Listen, I don't truck in that shit. *The Book of Veils,* all that. You want a German anti-tank mortar, I can help you out. But, like … devil books? That shit ain't me." Chris licked his lips; he was maybe a little more buzzed than he thought.

"You haven't heard my offer."

The passing streetlights spilled in his lap, ran up his chest, strobed past. Was it the drunkenness that made him ask? The cocksure quality in Pelletier's voice?

"What's your offer then?"

Pelletier didn't hesitate. "Twenty-five thousand dollars."

"Bullshit."

"I'm very serious. Twenty-five thousand dollars, for any edition, or an unauthorized reproduction."

Chris smiled. "Yeah, see, you don't strike me as the kind of guy with that kind of money, Edmund. Chinos hiked up to your tits, glasses all dirty. You look like you sleep in a fridge, dude."

"That's fair." He could hear the guy's smile on the other end of the line. "Maybe I find the trappings of the world—money, fashion —unimportant."

Chris took the on-ramp that would send him home. "Yeah, well. Like I said. I can't help you."

"I can be at your residence in twenty minutes with half the money. The other half upon receipt of the book."

"You're telling me you know where I live now?"

"Google is everyone's friend, Mr. Shaw."

Was it the fact that he'd just come from a session with his brothers? The memory of that perfect arc of his fist against that woman's jaw? How the beer twisted everything inside him?

"Okay," Chris said, calling him on his bluff. "You meet me in my driveway in twenty minutes with twelve thousand, five hundred dollars, I'll get you your fucking book."

He was surprised—and a little dismayed—to see Pelletier sitting in an idling sedan in his driveway. Chris parked his truck at the curb and walked over. Pelletier held out a padded envelope through the window. Chris reached for it, and then stopped. It was a hell of a lot of money, but did he actually *need* it? He was doing okay, wasn't he?

"I can see your misgivings, Mr. Shaw. There are other people I could contact. But I was told you're reputable. A man of your word."

"I am a man of my word."

"Well." Pelletier waggled the envelope towards him again.

"Thirty thousand."

Pelletier smiled. Smug and soft in his car, the stark contrast of his arms and that moon face of his against the sedan's dark interior. "Fine," he said. "But this is your down payment."

Chris took the envelope, thumbed through the stack of soft, worn hundreds. "Who do you work for, Edmund?"

Pelletier shrugged. "Those who are moved by your cause."

"Right," said Chris, walking towards his front door and thumbing the alarm on his truck with his key.

"Mr. Shaw," Pelletier called out, and Chris turned. "It's possible you might consider the book a debt I'm incapable of collecting. And I agree, I'm personally of no threat to you. But my employers, whose money you've just taken and to whom you're bound, are a different matter entirely."

"Yeah, see, that does sound like a threat to me, Edmund."

Pelletier held up his bone-white palms. "I'm just confirming the outlines of our agreement. You have my number. Collect the rest of your money, Mr. Shaw. Be wise, trust your instincts. Get the book, quickly, and call me when you have it." And with that and a fey smile that didn't touch the man's eyes at all, Pelletier backed out of the driveway.

CHRIS SLEPT for shit that night. He kept opening the drawer by his bedside to make sure the money was still there. And there was a not insignificant part of him that hoped it wouldn't be, that he'd dreamed the entire thing. But there it was. When he finally slept, he had panicked, watery dreams in which he called Pelletier and begged to give the money back, but Pelletier just kept drily chuckling and asking who was calling.

THE NEXT DAY, he called Mel Tucker and asked him out for a beer. Hungover and sweating, his heart just hammering in his chest. The dreams had thrown him, and he was certain by then that Pelletier was trouble, perhaps deadly trouble. Mel seemed surprised to hear from him—they knew a lot of the same people, went to the same rallies, posted on the same servers, but they weren't friends exactly, especially since Chris had splintered off from the Aryan Patriots the year before. Still, Mel said he could meet Chris for a pint at Mercy's that evening, a skinhead bar out in Vancouver.

That night he rolled up to Mercy's and was dismayed to see Mel crewed up, at least five other guys drinking with him in the back of the bar. He bought shots for Mel's guys first thing, starting the night out with some goodwill.

Finally, hours later, bleary-eyed with drink, Chris was able to get Mel alone in a booth. The other guys had either gone off to another bar or were over by the jukebox, running the pool table. Chris squinted one eye shut and focused on Mel's scarred, dented cue ball head, those four tears tattooed beneath his eye.

"I got a proposition for you," Chris said.

Mel grinned, showcasing a set of beautiful teeth greatly at odds with the rest of him. "You want your cap twisted, you got to talk to Robbie, bro. I don't play that song." He cupped his mouth with his hands. "Yo, Robbie! Shaw wants a date." Robbie waved Mel off, took his shot at the table.

"*The Book of Veils,*" Chris said. "You still got it?"

Mel pulled his head back, frowned. "I got it. Why?"

"I got someone wants to buy it."

Mel took a long pull from his Guinness, didn't break eye contact. Wiped foam from his mouth. "How much?"

"Five thousand dollars."

Mel got very still. "For me?"

"Yeah."

"How much do you get?"

"Five thousand."

"Shit," Mel said.

Chris said, "Hey, I'm the broker."

Mel rolled his head on his shoulders. "How much do you know about that book, Shaw?"

Here was Chris, playing nonchalant, playing like he wasn't panicked. Like those dreams last night hadn't rattled him hard. "I don't know. It was a book that Hitler commissioned towards the end of the war, when he started getting his ass handed to him. A collection of ... spells and incantations. Right? Occult stuff, meant to change the tide of the war." Chris drank deep from his own pint. "Not that it worked for shit."

Mel leveled a blunt finger at him. "First of all, talk about Daddy that way again and you'll be shooting your own teeth out of your dick, I promise you. Secondly, *Veils* is fucking deadly, Shaw. For real. I got a ripoff copy that some Austrians made in the sixties and I still keep that shit in a lead-lined box in my bunker. You know? Book's danger-ous. And it *wants* to be read, right? It messes with you. I read where one guy thinks there are actually *antifascist* incantations in there, things that could be used against us. It's fucked up. And it's sure as *shit* worth more than five thousand dollars."

"Well, what's reasonable, then?"

"You tell me," said Mel.

"Seven grand."

"Nah."

"Eight."

Mel shrugged, crossed those massive arms.

Chris made a face like it pained him. "I'll hit up my guy, tap him for a bit more. Ten thousand dollars, Mel. This has to happen."

Mel chewed on his cheek for a moment, uncrossed his arms and drummed his fingers on the table. "You know where the quarry is, Shaw?"

Chris nodded. "Yeah. Where the baby skins go to make their bones? Knock each other's teeth out and break bottles?"

Mel slid out of the booth. "Meet me there tomorrow night, ten o'clock. You bring all that money, Shaw, and I'll give you the book."

"What, we can't meet at your house? You don't trust me?"

Mel belched into his fist. "That's exactly right."

HE CALLED Pelletier's number from his truck and it went straight to a recording that said the owner of the number was unavailable, to leave a message.

"I'm working on it," Chris said. "I'm getting there."

His sleep was once again shotgunned through with nightmares. Pelletier with limbs bursting from the sleeves of his shirt, more limbs than belonged to ten men, wet and elongated and many-jointed, arms with claws, searching and blind.

CHRIS WALKED around the back of Mel's house at ten o'clock the next night. He'd been watching the place for the past two hours. Sure that somehow Mel would sense him burrowed in the loam in the copse of trees across from his place. Would sense that Chris had parked his truck a mile down the road and walked in. But no, 9:30 that evening, Mel had gotten in his own ride—a Honda Accord that fit him like a clown car—and driven away. Mel's house looked the same as it had during the few pre-rally warmups Chris had been to, back when he was still in good with the Aryan Patriots.

Mel's bunker was exactly that, an end-of-the-world scenario he'd paid big money for. Inset in the far corner of his backyard, it had big steel doors and concrete lining meant to alleviate any significant fallout from a nuclear event. Chris ran low along the side of the house with his duffel bag banging against his legs. A dog barked ferociously inside and Chris marveled at his good fortune. It was twenty minutes from here to the quarry; Chris figured Mel would wait for him maybe fifteen, twenty minutes, the promise of that money just too great. He had forty minutes to get the book.

Of course, if Mel had kept his word and actually brought the book to the quarry, everything was fucked.

His phone rang in his pocket. He crouched down next to the bunker's doors. "Yeah."

"He's here. He's got another guy with him," Mitch said. Mitch, on one of the mountains of shale, glassing the quarry with a night vision scope. "They're carrying, too."

Yeah, they were gonna roll him for the money. No way Mel had the book on him.

"I owe you," Chris said.

IT WAS A PADLOCK, decently sized, with a chain run through the bunker's door handles. His circular saw made short, if loud, work of the chain, and that was that. He unwound it, pulled open the doors, and stepped down into the bunker. Used his flashlight to look around. Neat and tidy, Nazi flags and SS banners hung on the cement walls. A rack of rifles, shelves of food and medical gear. Boxes of batteries. Mel the prepper.

On a desk, a steel bin slightly larger than a shoebox.

Tiny little padlock that his tin snips chewed through in a second. Easy.

He opened the lid and there was the book. A reproduction from the sixties, Mel had said, and still the cover looked like ... skin? Felt clammy to the touch when Chris picked it up? German lettering stacked on the cover in the manner of an illuminated manuscript, a prancing angel wending between the words, an angel that pulled its own jaw down into a scream. He should have been terrified, but he was not. He was exultant. It was a book that wanted you to read it, Mel had said, and he was right. It wanted you to partake.

He flipped through pages, marveled at the horrors.

Illustrations, photographs, incantations. Endless brutalities. He could not read German and yet entire threads of knowledge came to him and he began speaking them, rapturous. Urine sluiced hotly down his leg.

Chris lay his hand on a page and a paragraph's worth of words writhed and slid under his fingernails, burrowed under his skin, entered the jet stream of his screaming blood with something like ecstasy.

MEL CAME over to Chris's house later that night with two other men, all of them with long guns, and Chris held open the door for them. Two minutes later, his living room was a charnel house, Mel stabbed through the mouth and into the brain with one of the other men's femur. A loop of intestine swung merrily on the ceiling fan and Chris laughed and then gagged once, something dark and clotted falling from his lips, something that grew dozens of legs the moment it struck the blood-soaked carpet, something that set about feasting on the bodies.

HE CALLED Pelletier and made only a series of strange clicking noises, and Pelletier said warmly, "I'll be right there."

Pelletier stepped through the door and surveyed the carnage. He touched Chris on the cheek like a father would. Chris handed him the book without fanfare or longing. No money exchanged hands. Chris had already received his payment and his gift.

"It wants to be read, you understand," said Pelletier. "And Hitler was a fool. Thinking he was harnessing powers of darkness, when he was harnessing powers of light."

Chris nodded, clicked, dripped.

HE STOOD STILL in his room for days, not quite sleeping. Occasionally his children writhed from the mess in the living room and crawled up his body, entered his mouth and offered him sustenance. That Saturday he left his reeking, fly-clotted house and walked to the protest downtown. Walking by then was becoming difficult. Much of Chris's physiognomy had become blown out, distended, changed. He looked like a man long harried by wasps, lumped and bulbed. An ankle dragged on the pavement until the sock was worn away and a calligraphy-trail of blood was left behind, until finally he had worn it down to simple yellow tendon, and still he kept walking.

By late morning he had made it into downtown, threading his way through counter-protesters, which were a grand mishmash of Portlanders of every stripe—every skin tone, cultural affiliation, sexual identity. The disabled and sightless. Parents, grandparents, children. And yes, antifa. Black-clad men and women standing in loose formations, banners hung between some groups. And still Chris dragged himself onward. He was given a wide berth.

He crossed the police line between two cops bedecked in riot gear, beanbag shotguns hanging off their chests, and pulled himself into the fold of the far-right protesters. He passed among a phalanx of men dressed as gladiators, men who stood behind handmade shields with nails sticking out of them, men in vests and Pepe the Frog capes and shoulder pads, men who aimed paint guns at the other side of the police line and fired indiscriminately. Sieg heils and white power salutes popcorned among this side of the crowd. American flags, Gadsden flags, Confederate flags, swastikas all rippled in the wind. Body armor, banner poles that would double as weapons. Bear mace canisters held in the hands of dozens of people. There was Mitch, there was Big Jay, there was Pistol Mike. Chris was

hardly Chris anymore, and they looked at him with dark
wonderment.

There was Edmund Pelletier, further down the street, standing on
the lip of a fountain, which gave him an uncensored view of the
proceedings. He sipped a coffee. He wore dark glasses.

When Chris exploded in the midst of the fascist gathering, he did
so not in a gout of red mist, an explosion of gelled meat and liquified
organs, no. His explosion was one of prehensile, ancient limbs, limbs
with a mace-ball of claws at the end of each. Dozens of limbs, while
Chris himself was a skin that fell uselessly to the cement like a
discarded suit. What had been Chris was now a large writhing mass of
stick-like arms dripping with ichor and sinew, arms that ripped and
lurched through the crowd. Blood jetted in grand red splashes, heads
spun and bounced off the lower floors of the high rises there, the arms
roving among the top of the crowd like a nest of rats with their tails
tied together. Screams rippling for blocks. Police panicked, firing indiscriminately, hitting each other with impact munitions. A mass exodus,
chaos. Hundreds trampled. A man with a *Prepare the Ovens, Daddy
Trump* t-shirt screamed for his mother, while the beast used his
severed legs to skewer a skinhead's chest.

Pelletier stood on the lip of the fountain, sipping his coffee. He was
free, at least for the time being, of obligation. Death would come for
him eventually, but for now, he had fulfilled his responsibilities to the
forces of light that employed him.

There were, Pelletier understood, endless variants of what made a
man good or just. Morality was a fog in many ways. He knew it. He
believed it.

But the beasts couched in *The Book of Veils*? They were clear in their
delineations.

There were good people and bad people.

And then there were Nazis.

And Nazis, the beasts had made joyously clear, were motherfucking lunch.

HOSTILE ARCHITECTURE
BY M. LOPES DA SILVA

They just couldn't get enough sleep. They were always on their feet, walking. Until Ever's discount shoes were just strips of rubber. Their legs bundled wires. Their feet all raw blister. The city had gone vertical practically overnight. Not the buildings—Los Angeles couldn't be bothered to build upwards outside of the Downtown area—but everything else. All of the park bench seats were vertical now. The bus stop benches had developed an uncomfortable lean. And what couldn't be made vertical was punctured with enough spikes to make an iron maiden blush. The spikes were everywhere: on the gratings, on ground floor windowsills in skinny strips, tactfully concealed as little brass circles in store doorways by day and up like wardens at night. Lumpy boulders had replaced flat public patches of lawn, and every flat place was policed. If there weren't security guards around ready to move them on, there were the cops. And the cops were always eager to sweep the tent camps on the sidewalks, hassle the folks sleeping there, detain them and throw their possessions away—medications, licenses, bedding—because everything on the sidewalk was garbage to these city employees who'd vowed to keep the streets clean.

But they weren't garbage. They were people: angry, exhausted, restless people. People who couldn't sleep, who weren't being allowed to sleep.

Sleep deprivation does funny things to the mind. It intensifies things. Draws pictures in the gaps of information that start to occur as the brain randomly turns off and on again. Off, and on again.

A September night in Los Angeles: copper light on low clouds. Off.

Standing in front of a trash can fire behind the long-closed diner, Ever had a vision. An ecstasy. Things unfolded and kept unfolding. First fluffy pages of tissue paper and unwanted mailers curling, charring, then the edges of the graffitied walls. The holes in between the chain-link fence. The light of distant stars smeared by smog. An angel formed within the flames, a thousand mouths smiling. Sparks wept from her lone eye. She extended her endlessly long arms towards them and caressed the topmost curve of their left cheek. Ever could smell the downy fuzz there burn away at her touch.

Her mouths were whispering, but they were talking all at once, and Ever was having difficulty understanding. They wanted to understand. They wanted to know.

"Please," Ever said, "I don't know what you're saying. Tell me so I can understand."

The mouths went silent into smiles, then began again, in unison this time:

Wield.

AND ON AGAIN.

Ever stood in front of a YIELD sign posted next to a freeway on-ramp. It was late, and cold. They were alone. Not even a rat in the weeds. Ever shivered, then reached for a permanent marker that they kept in their coat pocket, uncapped it, and changed "YIELD" to "WIELD" with two quick marks. They stared at their edit. Pocketed their pen.

On top of the WIELD sign a strip of long spikes was affixed; even

the birds in the city were denied rest. The spikes were awkwardly
attached, half-falling from the top of the sign already even though they
looked relatively new. Ever reached up and touched the very tip of one
of the thin, nail-like spikes and flinched at its sharpness. Then they
reached for the base, the metallic strip part, and pulled a little—it was
loose. Slowly Ever peeled the strip free from the sign, careful not to
cut themselves. When they were done, they held the weaponized
metal ribbon tautly before them. A distant traffic light changed and
spilled some red on the spikes.

The tips of the spikes danced, moving with the tremor of Ever's
hands. They had never been able to stand the sight of blood. The
thought of pain.

THEY TRIED TO SLEEP.

They found a rare clear pocket under a freeway—sheltered from
the weather and prying eyes alike. Unclaimed and dry. Ever could
hardly believe their luck. They sat down, their back against the wall,
knees up to their chest, hands in their coat pockets. They tried to
ignore the piercing cold shooting up through the bottom of their jeans
from the asphalt. It wasn't too hard; they were tired enough.

Off.

Darkness and flames. The fires drifted, twisting with hypnotic soft-
ness, becoming her again. The angel. Sparks wept from her eye. They
blushed. They felt a sudden and intense desire seize them – they
wanted to kiss the face of the burning angel whose infinite lips parted
to whisper, once more:

Wield.

A cop was there.

For no real reason so far as Ever could tell, a cop was just suddenly
standing in the middle of their erotic dream. They couldn't understand
what he was saying. His words were overlapping, garbled. It sounded
like they were coming from very far away. And then he reached down
to touch them.

Ever whipped their right fist straight up into the cop's gut, not removing it from their coat pocket.

Ever laughed. Whipped cream was inexplicably spilling out of the cop's stomach, soaking into their coat and getting their fist sticky. The cop was making funny faces. They removed their fist from their pocket and saw part of the spike strip wrapped around it, pointy part outwards, covered with sugary white goop.

Ever shoved the goopy fist into the cop's face, and he stopped making funny faces, which was good because they were grossing Ever out.

And on again.

Blood everywhere. Flashing red and blue lights. Ever screamed. Off.

They fell.

It was dark and their legs suddenly couldn't support them so they fell. Their head banged against the pavement. Their bottom teeth pierced their tongue and they recoiled against the fresh blood abruptly filling their mouth, then the back of their throat. They were choking on it.

Another cop came out of the car. He had a gun pointed at them.

Ever was there. Ever wasn't there. Ever was choking on blood. The cop came close, reached out to touch them.

Now Ever's left fist came up and connected with this cop's gut and his gun went off—too close to Ever's head—but the shot whined wide into the wall. And Ever's left fist kept connecting. And connecting. And connecting. Because their dream had turned nightmare and there was a body on top of them that they did not want and it kept moving, it kept moving and should not be moving at all. Their left hand was wet. Warm. They gripped the other half of the spike strip so tightly that the edges of the ribbon cut into their palm. When the body finally went still and Ever could hear things again they heard a chime, a note so lyrical and pure that it could have been the voice of an angel singing in Ever's ears.

They shoved the cop's body off of them and stood, spitting out blood, looking for her. Only the red and blue lights were there. The two bodies on the ground. The distant song of a siren.

Ever followed the torch song.

DAWN DESATURATED THE NIGHT.

A project: a real divine DIY. Ever was preoccupied with it; inspiration was truly everywhere. Ever wandered by a pile of abandoned furniture heaped up on the curb. A mattress had been left out overnight and the dew that had collected there was steaming off in a funk that Ever could visibly see, and therefore steered clear of. Next to the mattress was the broken iron frame of a bed, partially disassembled and jutting out awkwardly into the street.

Ever walked over to the iron frame and pulled one of the long, unbent bars free. Bounced it in their hands. Hefted it up in the air experimentally.

A security door rattled. Someone exited from a nearby apartment. Ever was already walking away with the iron bar held close to their body, their heart pounding too loud for their liking, their calves screaming for them.

THE DAY HAD DEVELOPED A FLICKER.

The flicker wasn't always there, only sometimes. A little shadow lurking in the middle of the light. A dark rim around people like an outline or an aura. Electricity was louder. Their knuckles kept creeping up to insulate their ears from the constant buzz that leaked from light sockets and hummed in the power lines.

They just couldn't get enough sleep. They tried to buy a cup of coffee and sit down at a fast food place that usually let Ever in but the cashier, Joan, said that her boss was watching today. New policy: you had to buy food to sit down at the tables. Ever understood perfectly.

They ordered their coffee to go. They wanted to laugh; they couldn't, but they wanted to. Joan kept looking at them funny.

The caffeine felt like nothing. Like pouring water into the sea. Ever drank it down to the dregs. Kept walking. Kept listening to that song they couldn't quite make out. Followed it up and down the long blocks of Los Angeles.

Kept ducking into alleys to work on their craft project.

A DISTANT ROAR, soft cheering and applause rebounded along the asphalt and concrete. Ever blinked at the echoes. It sounded like a speaker system. Muffled booming words were punctuated with more applause. Were they all witnessing the angel's glory? They hugged their craft project to their chest and followed the sounds, found a big crowd. Hovered at the edge of it.

A politician was speaking. Some recently elected mayor or governor in an expensive brown suit. Flashes went off from the gaggle of professional and amateur photographers in the crowd gathered around him.

"We're working hard to keep the homeless off of our streets. To protect our hard-working, tax-paying families from being exposed to—"

That was one voice. The politician's voice. But Ever heard another voice singing through the sound system, speaking from multiple mouths. A holy voice. They just had to get closer to hear it better. To understand.

Ever looked around. The speakers were mounted on top of flat truck beds. They picked one of the trucks and started heading towards it, pushing through the throngs of people. At first it was difficult, but once people started to notice the bloodstains they gave them more room. When they reached the truck, however, they encountered some resistance.

A security guard leaned against the truck, his gym-puffed muscles folded across his chest.

"Where do you think you're going?"

Ever blinked at him. Took a step towards the truck bed. The guard unfolded his arms and shoved against the center of Ever's chest.

Ever launched their craft project up from its hiding place by their left armpit and a long iron javelin scraped to a fine stabbing point pierced the underside of the guard's jaw and exited the top of his skull. Just the tip of the javelin jutted up, like the tiniest black bird beak in a nest of crushed brain and hair. Ever regretted that they had nothing to feed it.

Other people were shouting, raising phones, standing back. They were just more voices to ignore in a sea of noise. Ever removed the holy javelin from the guard's head and mounted the truck bed. Pressed their head against the speakers' foam to catch the buzzing, whispering, crackling voices leaking from them.

"I'm listening," Ever said. "I want to understand."

"An eyesore that lowers the property values of our homes—" said the speaker.

And the angel's voice, there but undiscernible, buried beneath so much sound.

Ever trembled. The people standing closest to the truck were making strange faces. They hefted their holy javelin and stared at the politician, whose useless words kept getting in the way. They thought they might be close enough now to be understood.

Heat surged through Ever, elevating their spine, bracing their arms. Sparks wept from the pores on their forearms, singeing the hair there. They were smoking, blazing, launching their iron javelin through the air on a sacred flight that ended spiking the politician right through the middle, pinning him backwards to the earth. Bright confetti fistfuls of his blood were everywhere. Ever laughed and laughed because the blood kept changing color like a beautiful party trick.

THE EDGES of the world were curling, burning. Ever could see the angels standing in the crowd, their clothing worn out, their eyes undying flames. In between the screaming, panicked people, the divine were watching. Waiting for their chance to catch fire.

And on and on again.

RED BRICK
BY CYNTHIA GÓMEZ

Bill was certain he'd locked the door. He always did as soon as he got back in the house, no matter what purpose had drawn him outside. He'd drilled this knowledge into his kids, his wife Lauren, the Mexican woman that Lauren brought in to clean once a week: lock the door, always, every time. Because these days, you just never know.

But somebody had failed, somebody had shirked their duty, because there was the back door yawning open—no, gaping—and in front of it there was a man. Dark brown skin in a shirt the color of a dirty brick, just sitting at Bill's kitchen table, Thanksgiving turkey leg greasing his chin, the hanging lamp casting shadows on his sweaty face.

Bill's hand went to his waist for the gun that wasn't there, the one that right this second was locked in the safe two rooms away. The stranger didn't move, didn't blink, just stared at Bill's frame blocking the door to the hallway, the door that led to the rest of the house. The eyes were inscrutable, black and glistening like the fat on his hands from the turkey leg, the last one left from yesterday, the one he had promised to save for his wife. Bill felt revulsion cross over his face, and something else like a live wire stabbed at his brain, flashing away too fast to be caught. The man stood up and Bill crossed the distance between them before he could think, reaching for the red shirt that was already gone, that had already slipped out the open door and beyond the reach of the back porch light.

He spent the next hour with his flashlight and his sidearm at his hip, trampling Lauren's poppy beds over and over, checking every single board in the back fence, looking for one that was loose or crumbling or had telltale signs of digging underneath. Everything was as it should be. He wanted to look in the yard next door and even considered waking the neighbors, but his Spanish was little more than a collection of commands, and that was all they seemed to speak. He'd never been able to keep straight who was the father over there; there were about two or three men and women and as many packs of children, sweet little things who squealed in delight on sunny afternoons in the spray from their garden hose.

The next morning while Lauren made breakfast he asked everyone about it in turn, mentioning the gaping door but not the intruder. Amber was, at fifteen, definitely old enough to know better; so was Mason, who at eleven knew he was the deputy man of the house, who even wore a little Deputy badge that Bill pinned on him whenever he had to work late or be out of town for a weekend. Lauren knew how to handle a gun and how to aim at a threat, but Bill realized soberly how she could be overwhelmed; she was the kind of woman who'd be trying to take out the trash while calling Mason's school while pulling out weeds from the yard. "We all make mistakes," he insisted after each of them had denied it in turn. "The important thing is to own up to them and not let them define you." Lauren raised her eyebrow at this last one, and he had to admit to himself, it was a bit much. It was useless anyway; they hadn't left the door unlocked, they were certain, all three of them. Finally he had to let it go and let the kids disappear into their rooms.

Lauren squeezed his shoulders and opened the fridge. "Hey babe, I can't find the last drumstick. Did you clean the fridge or something?" She liked to change the subject by talking about food, but of course she didn't know she was bringing the subject right back. He'd have to fall on the sword if he didn't want to terrify her.

"I'm sorry, I ... you know, midnight munchies and all."

"But you said you were leaving it for me."

The puzzlement and hurt scored her face, but he preferred it to the fear that it was his job to keep from her. She shoved aside boxes and jars until she found the tupperware she'd packed on Thursday evening, tipsy from the last of the Yellowtail. The container held a single drumstick, swaddled in the layers and layers of plastic wrap she always used. He swallowed hard, rolling the straw place mat in his hands, and then walked away from her face and headed straight for the shower, turning up the water hotter than he ever had.

It happened again that afternoon. Lauren was taking Amber to swim practice and Mason was shooting hoops in the driveway; Bill was waiting for the contractor he'd called out to install a second gun safe, tucked away in the pantry two steps from the back door. The company would come the next day to install cameras and alarms, and he'd have to find some way to justify to Lauren the expense of an installation on Sunday of Thanksgiving weekend. Bill opened the door to wave goodbye to his wife and daughter as they drove off, and the smile bounced right back off of his face as he saw those same cheap sneakers, those tan pants splotched with grease, that red shirt with a dark patch that looked like sweat spreading across the chest. No sign of a weapon in his hands. The man was right next to the path of the van, but Lauren was looking behind her as she always did, trained harder than instinct to look for a child in her rearview, thinking more of the danger she might pose than what was lurking in front of her.

"Mason, get in the house."

The boy looked at his father, startled, blessedly not looking behind him to where the threat loomed. Bill crossed the walkway and pushed his son back inside, putting his body between his boy and danger.

"Dad, what the—"

"Just trust me. Get in your room. Don't come out until I tell you." Bill glanced over his shoulder once, twice; the stranger was standing stock-still at the edge of the driveway, an expression on his face that looked like nothing so much as a smirk. He'd beat this man bloody or blow holes in him, whichever the moment called for. The flash ran through his brain again, just out of reach, an echo of dirty shoes slapping pavement. Bill pushed his son through the open door and the second Mason disappeared down the hallway Bill grabbed the metal bat that stood by the door and spun around. The walkway was empty; the driveway was clear.

Bill made Mason stay in his room while he walked the entire perimeter twice, the bat swapped out for the pistol, not responding to the texts Lauren sent: *Mason said you snapped at him? You were doing so much better, whats wrong?* He didn't like this triangulation, and it was worse when Amber sent him a gif of a burly man breathing deeply on a yoga mat. He wanted a picture of the intruder so he could send it to his family: *this is what I protect you from.* But he'd never do that; it was his job to bear this fear so that they could sleep easy at night. His heart didn't stop lurching until the contractor pulled up.

Then came Amber's swim meet against St. John three days later. The last heat, which she was primed to win. He was sitting on the bleachers at one end of the pool, fighting sleep, lulled and then jerking awake at the elegance of those shapes cutting through the depths, arms slicing through and returning with no wasted motion, the bodies staying effortlessly in their lanes when a simple distraction, a simple slip of attention and focus, would have sent them colliding, with so much at stake. He wondered if their coaches made them practice without the lane markers, where their bodies could learn the practice of keeping their place. He found Amber's flowered cap streaming towards the finish line, flicked his eyes up to the time clock on the wall and there, maybe ten feet away from his daughter, the stranger's feet perched at the edge of the concrete, pool water in a puddle around those cheap shoes.

Bill stood up and his jacket swung at Lauren's face. "What are you doing? Amber's almost—" and the cheers were already interrupting her, Amber climbing out of the blue as the announcer called out her first-place finish and Coach Graham draped a towel around her shoulders and the stranger loomed just behind them both. Bill shoved through the crowd and over to his daughter, fists already forming; people stepped out of his way as soon as they glimpsed his face, casting their eyes behind them to see what could have earned that expression. Bill pulled Amber toward him with a sharp yank on her elbow, ignoring her yelp of pain; he'd apologize later, she'd understand.

The stranger walked directly in front of Coach and waved a brown hand back and forth in front of those green eyes, eyes that didn't react, didn't blink, that never took their gaze from Bill's fists.

Bill let himself turn to see Amber, still rubbing her arm. Lauren was watching from across the pool. Coaches, assistants, Amber's friends, looking up from their phones or each other, questions unspoken on their faces, and not one of them casting a glance at a stranger in a red shirt, smirk widening above that greasy chin, so clearly not belonging, but drawing not a single look.

THEY WERE NEARLY HALFWAY home from St. John before Lauren switched off the Tom Petty and turned to him. "So are we going to talk about what happened back there?" She was driving, which she was usually only too happy to let him do. The back seat was empty; Lauren had got one of Amber's friends to take her home from the meet. East 14th streamed past them in the chill. The sky was threatening rain. He'd have to remember to cover up the metal chairs in the backyard or the next guests would be sitting on a coating of rust.

"Bill?" He hadn't heard that tone in forever. The van idled at a light, and Bill closed his eyes, wondering: if he opened them, would he find the stranger leaning towards the window, grinning and invisible to everyone else?

"Did something happen at work?" Her question seemed to snap his eyes open, and he clamped his hands over them both, rubbing his eyes to cover up the sudden motion.

"Something always happens at work. It's not like I work at a shoe store."

"You know what I mean. Is this about that raid? At the restaurant? I thought you'd gotten over that."

The wire snagged again, live and crackling. A Mexican restaurant, a young man scurrying out the kitchen door against Bill's approaching steps, red shirt stained with sweat.

"I hate it when you call it that. I don't raid anything. I carry out apprehension actions against criminal aliens."

"Oh, so your buddies can call it that, but I can't?"

"What are you talking about?"

"You think I can't hear you when you and Alan and José Luís joke about stocking up on Raid?"

"Those two say that. Not me."

"That's not better. And am I really going to have this conversation with you keeping your hands on your eyes the whole time?"

"Notice you didn't ask what's wrong with them? What if I have an eye infection?"

"Please. If you did, nobody would hear the end of it. You're a big old tough guy until you get sick. So I guess I'm getting the Bill Special. You'll talk about what you want, when you want to?"

"You know, this is really making me feel better here. Thanks."

"Better?" She said it like it was a brand new word he'd dug out of the mud. He felt the car round the last corner to home, under the wheels the cracking concrete of the driveway he'd been meaning to fix.

"And will you look at me while you talk, for fuck's sake?" She never swore either. He let his hands fall away, one at a time, opening his eyes in little sips, but there was nothing out there. She turned off the car.

"You know I had a hard time making peace with your job. But I told myself someone's got to do it, and that you can set a good example for all those knuckleheads coming up under you. And it was okay. But the agreement was always: you left work at work. Not make us deal with it too. This isn't the first time you've gone back on it. Is it going to be the last?"

Bill's head jerked toward a movement in the darkness, a small furry movement with orange stripes, dashing under the hedges. His relief came out in a laugh that was almost a cough. Lauren snatched her keys from the ignition and slammed the car door, her shape blurring as frost overtook the window glass.

That night he stretched out on the couch, a single broken spring digging into his back, and at some point he must have slept because he saw Amber at the edge of the pool, suited up and ready to go, bathing cap snugly in place, and when she went to jump in he saw that the lane markers were rows of sneakers, cheap Keds interspersed with work boots caked in mud, and tiny shoes gleaming white like baby teeth. He screamed and went to pull her back, and her bathing suit was the color of a dirty brick and soaked in blood.

He lay awake for three hours after that until the darkness began to lift from the sky. His head felt like a rock, cracking in the sun, but he splashed water on his face and drove the Silverado to their favorite donut shop. He snapped on the radio and began singing along almost without thought, tapping the steering wheel as Phil sang about what was coming in the air.

He'd have just enough time to drop them off before work: a maple bar for Amber and the rainbow sprinkles that Mason and Lauren both loved. Mason would forgive the snap and Amber the humiliation in front of her friends and Lauren the breaking of his promise, again, the glue again knitting together the broken pieces. He pulled into the lot and turned off the Silverado.

The stranger was standing next to the passenger door.

The next seconds would replay over and over in Bill's head when he least wanted them to, and when he slid into the driver's seat of a car—any car—or closed his hand around a set of keys, he would over and over again see himself dropping the keys with a shriek that sounded like a teenage girl, fumbling desperately under the seat, grazing a litter of old fries and gum wrappers but nothing metal, even though he'd heard them drop, they had to be there, fingers slipping over pencils and napkins and finally stabbing at the keys, dropping them again before he jammed them into the ignition and peeled off, and he was already streaming along Callan Avenue when he saw it, traced by a brown finger into the frosted window of the passenger side: BOO.

"You all right, man?" Bill's boss leaned into the doorway, taking in the empty packets of Excedrin in the wastebasket, the cardboard cups in a long row between them on the metal desk, each one thicker with sugar and Coffee Mate, the wall clock that barely read 6:54.

"It's nothing. Lauren." His voice cracked at her name. Alan nodded. Nothing new here, his nod said. Bill's stomach rumbled; all morning, anything he'd tried to eat called up those dirty fingers on the window and his own hands, useless and fumbling.

"Hey, man, you ever need counseling, there's always the EAP." He said this the way you'd talk about going to the dentist.

"Yeah, sure. Hey, you remember that raid last month?" In Alan's face Bill could see a whole wall of gears unused to turning.

"That apartment complex? With the woman who wouldn't shut up?"

"No, the restaurant, the one in Fruitvale. The runner."

"They're all runners. What's up?"

"Do we have any pictures of him?" Those dirty sneakers slapping pavement as Bill pulled out his gun. That terrified face, turning back to Bill and his gun, not seeing the alley opening up to East 8th, the cars rushing to beat the light.

"Pictures? Oh, you mean that poor bastard. No, he wasn't even a target. County would have the autopsy photos though. What's left, anyway, after that van fucked him up. You okay, man?"

When Amber was scared, she clung to her mother; Lauren would let herself crumple against Bill, every part of her softening against his bulk. He'd long since told Mason that men had to be made of stronger stuff. What would happen if right now Bill opened his arms wide, if he let his boss feel the shaking that would not stop, if he spilled out the story of the man he had to bear all by himself, the fear he longed to set down for just one second? What would Alan do, this man who would yank off the lights in detention cells when the prisoners whined too hard about the cold?

The laughter cracked open Bill's face. When it finally died he stood up and squeezed past Alan into the hall, ignoring the wheels grinding in his boss' face. He could hear the sound of chairs in the meeting room scraping the floor, voices beginning to fill the room for shift meeting, the room filling with the smell of weak coffee just beginning to burn.

Ten feet down the hall, maybe twenty, the stranger was walking. Nobody was supposed to be anywhere on this floor without authorization, those key cards with the awful pixelated photos on the front. And still here the man was, that brick-red shirt blooming with blood, his pant legs shredded and a tire mark running along his left side. And he was headed for the room full of Bill's coworkers, not a one of them seeming to notice the danger, this man smirking his way through their space. Bill was the only thing between the intruder and them. He slowly unholstered his gun, aiming for the tire mark on the left knee, the barrel dipping wildly under his shaking hands, and behind him Alan's voice rising: "Bill. Bill, what the fuck are you doing?"

He couldn't turn around and take his eyes off the threat. He couldn't advance; that might only provoke. And he couldn't let off a shot, not in this narrow space where it could ricochet back on anyone, including Bill himself. He could hear chairs being pushed back, the voices quieting behind him. But not a single gun being unholstered against the danger, no one shouting out to that smirking face to freeze or get down. Just the silence of a room of men holding their breath. And then Alan's hand closing around the gun, pulling it from Bill's hand, and the sound of a morning's worth of coffee and Excedrin and last night's Laphroaig splattering onto the floor. Bill's eyes shot up wildly, away from the vomit coating his hands (empty things scrabbling) and back down the hall, and the stranger was walking away, no one even trying to follow.

Alan was going to usher Bill into his office now. He would offer a short leave, stress relief, and Bill would have to tell him about this man who couldn't be real, but who had to be real, had to, because otherwise nothing else was.

Bill walked away from his boss, away from all of them. He'd call Alan later. The door buzzed meekly as he pulled it shut.

If he and Lauren had been talking, she might have asked him about the gas. Once Alan put him on leave he began to fill the Silverado's tank every other day instead of twice a week, driving endless miles every day until his usual time to come home, running up the charges on their shared Visa bill. If she noticed, she said nothing. She was never close enough to him to smell the endless cups of sugary coffee on his breath, and she wouldn't see the Red Bull he'd stashed three cases deep in the back seat. She never checked the car, never even drove it without his permission, not after the time he'd shouted at her in the driveway about scraping the paint. The only things she asked about were bland and unimportant: could he make the meeting with Mason's teacher; would he call his insurance about the kids' orthodontist bill; don't forget about Amber's recital—what do you mean you have to work?

The stranger didn't come back. Every day Bill just pointed the Silverado down a different street and then drove anywhere he could navigate without thinking, Michael Savage on the radio, volume turned half down but the anger seeping through the speaker anyway. Lauren hated that kind of radio, and normally he played it only to needle her, but something about the spikes and peaks of outrage were soothing, jolting him upright just when the car threatened to veer over the lines. Once he scraped right against the sidewalk where a woman was walking with her two kids. She had the same deep brown skin as the stranger, even had the man's same expression. They always had that same expression: blank, inscrutable, holding something back, some misguided effort at dignity, like Bill was the one in the wrong, like they weren't trespassing in someone else's country.

The day finally came for him to go back to work, and the stranger was still gone. His alarm woke him the same time as always, but his head hurt worse than it ever had, like his brain was hurling itself against the thick walls of his skull, and the lines that had always been there were instead nothing but cracks, from the inside, like an egg. His forehead knocked at the bottle of Laphroig he'd shoved under the sofa cushions, where Lauren wouldn't see it whenever she walked past him, observing him while he pretended to sleep. How many nights had he slept there? Had they even spoken yesterday?

He looked over to the tall window next to the front door, and through his half-closed eyes he saw it, motion where none had been, breaking the pristine circle of light at the edge of the driveway that kept the darkness at bay.

He was up. He pulled the gun from where he'd been keeping it on top of the TV cabinet, yanking the front door open with a slam against the garage wall, to where the dirty brick shirt blocked his path, flowering with blood that stained the edges of the greasy hair, the heart in the middle like an illegal bulls-eye, and before he even realized he'd pulled the trigger the shots rang out on the street and his cracked voice along with them: "Fuck you, you greaser piece of shit! Leave my family alone!" The street was empty and the lights snapping on all around him looked like eyes, like bloodshot eyes prying open. Opening in a row, the cul-de-sac lighting up, himself at the base of it, white shirt stained with yellow under the arms.

Bill wasn't going to wait for what was coming. He threw himself into the Silverado and peeled off, and before he even hit the lights of the Bay Bridge Alan had called him three times, the last time leaving a voicemail that Bill played and replayed as he headed west. "Bill, Lauren called me, and she's very concerned. She's talked to some neighbors who ... anyway, we need to talk. I'm going to meet you in the garage when you get here. Please call me back." The sun glinted off the surrounding car windows as it rose, and for a terrible few seconds the brightness was all he could see.

He'd ended up in the wrong lane, the one with toll takers instead of FasTrak, and there was no time to shove through the bollards and into the right one. He sighed and slid $10 out of his pocket for the toll. What the hell, he'd let the toll taker keep the change. It was the tiniest gestures of kindness that made the world go round.

He slowed and stuck his hand out the window. The toll taker grinned, brick-red shirt soaked with blood, greasy hands reaching into the space between them.

THE FOUR MAGI OF MOTAKWA COUNTY

BY MAX D. STANTON

1867

"Blood sacrifice is the only principle that can hold a civilized people together," proclaimed Eli Cawbridge, the Exalted Cyclops of Motakwa County. "In the end, it all comes down to blood—the foundation of all power, from the crucifixion of Jesus to the rights of kings. Even the red stripes in the Union flag stand for blood." His three confederates listened closely. They sat on horseback, clad in their white hoods and robes. Before them, a brutalized body dangled from the crooked young oak at Billing's farm. "Do you feel that?" Cawbridge asked his accomplices. "That rush of energy in your veins? The sweet voices beckoning?"

"I feel like I could do anything at all," said one of the masked four, his soft, drawling voice charged with sinister dreaminess. "I've never felt so alive. Not when my children were born. Not even at the Battle of Richmond." Another murmured in affirmation.

"This is what happens when the right blood feeds the right soil," Cawbridge said. "I tell you, this homely spot is a place of power. The ley lines intersect here and the Earth itself thirsts for death. Like the groves of the druids, or the pyramids of pagan Mexico, or Golgotha itself. And Motakwa County has many places like this, gentlemen. This is old, rich land. There are so many Golgothas here, waiting for us to make use of them." Cawbridge was a preacher by trade. Each of his fellow Klansmen had heard him speak of Golgotha before, and considered him an authority on the subject.

"What do you propose?" asked one of the murderers, his white hood and gown speckled red.

"I have mapped the ley lines of Motakwa County," said Cawbridge. "I say that we four take control of them, using human sacrifices and graven images to stake our claims. The Yankees will never touch us again, not with such elemental forces at our backs. We'll be free to run this county the right way. The old-fashioned way. Old-fashioned as Atlantis."

"Blood magic is a dangerous affair," cautioned one of the masked men, a Freemason who, like Cawbridge, had found the fraternity a stepping stone into terrorism and the occult. "The powers we tap into will also tap into us," he said.

"Would you have it any other way?" Cawbridge asked.

2021

ELI CAWBRIDGE IV stood at his pulpit, looking out over his well-scrubbed and prosperous flock. He enjoyed the shepherd's role. To his point of view he kept his people safe from outside harm or corruption, and thus they were his to do with as he pleased. That was how he'd been raised. He took a deep breath and launched into the day's sermon, on the theme of respect for tradition.

After the service was over Eli went downstairs to the church basement, seeking the Sunday's true spiritual refreshment. For more than a hundred and fifty years the basement of the Redeemer's Baptist Church had served as the ritual lodge for the white mages of Motakwa County. A great number of the county's unsolved murders, disappearances, and unexplainable phenomena had their beginnings and endings in this well-secured little klavern. In accord with the quasi-Masonic numerology that the lodge's founder practiced, they arranged their dealings in fours. Four directions of the compass, four sides of the square, four Gospels of the Bible, four arms of the swastika. Four was deemed a strong man's number.

Racks of weaponry stood all along the west wall. You could trace the progress of American mayhem from the Civil War through the present on that wall, from a Henry repeating rifle that had taken lives at Bull Run all the way to a gleaming new AR-15 that had taken lives at a high school. This was the domain of the Knight of the Sword, Raymond Lee Schultze. In addition to his membership in this lodge he was also an initiate of the Aryan Nations, and he had tattooed himself with their signs and symbols to permanently sever himself from all constraints of ordinary society. Like a werewolf, he had changed his skin to become superhumanly ferocious, but unlike a werewolf he could never transform back to a human being.

Paintings and photographs of the lodge's former members hung on the eastern wall, looking down on the deeds of their successors. This was the domain of the Knight of the Pure Blood, Fred Vanderman. Pleasant, soft-spoken Fred Vanderman was president of the school board, the historical society, and the chamber of commerce, with a side interest in ritualistic serial killing. His necromancy twisted memories and forgettings. He mutilated the past to bend the present and future to his liking.

The north side of the chamber was decorated with an enormous psychographic map of Motakwa County, marking all its criss-crossing ley lines and etheric currents in minute detail. This direction belonged to Arlen Clemmer, the Knight of the Threshold, who also held the title of county sheriff. Sheriff Clemmer's magic was strongest at borders and in-between places. He kept people where they were supposed to be. He ruled over the roads. He excelled at disappearances.

Finally, flags hung all along the southern wall, a United Nations of white nationalism. The stars and stripes, its blue-striped twin, the

Confederate battle flag, the swastika, the Gadsden coiled rattlesnake, the call to Make America Great Again, and a number of esoteric militia insignia all stood on proud display, each representing the sigil of an invisible spirit that offered men power and meaning in exchange for their souls. Portraits of Christ and Baphomet, each of whom the cultists invoked for separate purposes, hung at opposite sides. This was Eli Cawbridge's domain. For four generations the Cawbridge men had plumbed the most violent and atavistic depths of the subconscious mind, refining its seething murk into gold. His diabolical alchemy transmuted the base matter of human cruelty into nations and doctrines and armies. He was the Knight of the Banner. By his own reckoning he was the heart of the lodge, but each of the Knights felt likewise about their own portfolio.

After the white wizards donned their robes and pointed hoods, they chanted ritual oaths of allegiance and sang songs in honor of their ancestors. They then attended to the constant spiritual warfare that was the business of their lodge. The Knight of the Pure Blood said that evil was loose upon the land. He'd seen visions of social justice warriors organizing, and of the sinister daemons Seearti and ACAB worming into the minds of children. The Knight of the Sword spat out a curse, hissing obscenities so vile they turned the air around his lips to smoke and ash. The Knight of the Banner proposed a sacrifice along Billing Road. Maybe a traffic stop gone bad. The Knight of the Threshold said that he would take care of it once Mercury was in the proper alignment.

Their ceremony complete, the magi returned to their homes, happy and comfortable in their dominion.

That night, unknown vandals toppled the statue of Stonewall Jackson on Winston Boulevard, which was both the spot where six invisible ley lines converged and the dividing line that separated the town's White and Black neighborhoods. The iconoclasts dragged the monument from its pedestal and crushed its head with a sledgehammer, scattering gravel across the asphalt.

That same night, Sheriff Clemmers' wife Trudy found the Knight of the Threshold dead in his living room. He lay stiffly on a white shag carpet dyed dark red, his head caved in, as if from repeated hammer blows.

WITH THE MONUMENT DESTROYED, the polarity of Motakwa County's psychic energy reversed sharply, which was exactly what the monument had been designed to prevent. South of Winston Boulevard, fevered rumors flew about antifa death squads. There were long lines at the gun stores and short tempers in the bars. Residents of the north part of town hunkered in much as they would for a hurricane, avoiding the roads if they could. Yet behind closed doors, there was a quiet sense of relief. Toasts were drunk to Arlen Clemmer's eternal damnation, and to Stonewall Jackson's, too.

Eli typically loved burials. To his tongue, funeral fried chicken tasted finer than any other sustenance. However, the preacher had no joy planting Arlen Clemmers in the ground. He'd known Arlen since they were kids. They used to watch football together in the very living room where Arlen's head exploded. With the Lodge reduced to three members Eli no longer felt like a proper shepherd, but like a table with one of its legs removed. He wondered if any of Clemmer's deputies possessed the mettle to make a replacement. After the funeral, Eli slipped away to the church basement to confer with his brothers. They were already in full regalia when he arrived.

"What the hell happened?" the Knight of the Sword asked.

"A magician murdered Arlen," said Eli. "Whoever did this knew that Arlen had tied his life force to Stonewall's statue. They toppled the monument because they knew it would kill the man."

"What if they were just worthless little shitstains out to desecrate our history?" the Knight of the Pure Blood suggested. "They might not have known what they were doing. Maybe they got lucky."

"No sir. Absolutely not. Our order exists to control the luck around these parts. No antifa's going to catch a break in Motakwa County. The killer shouldn't have been able to so much as lay hands on that monument without suffering a stroke. We're dealing with a hermetic assassination."

"Who could have done this?" the Knight of the Sword asked, seething with rage.

"If I knew he'd be dead already," said the preacher. "I can't scry worth a damn anymore. All that energy we were channeling is running wild."

"I'm putting all my men on this," the Knight of the Sword growled. "This is war."

"It's always war," said Eli. "Always. Peace is the price of power, don't ever forget that. Not that I think you would."

"But how do we find the killer?" the Knight of the Pure Blood asked.

"Why, that'll be the easy part," Eli replied. "We know where the son of a bitch is going to strike. He's coming for us on our home turf. The little coward got Arlen by surprise, but that trick can't work more than once. We three are going to catch this animal, and once we've got him we will use his blood and pain to initiate a new Knight of the Threshold and make our lodge whole again."

FRED VANDERMAN, the Knight of the Pure Blood, had bound his soul to Darrow House, a delicately preserved plantation manor nestled by a stream lined with cypress trees and weeping willows. Fred traced his own genealogy back through this very mansion and his great-grandmother Martha Darrow. He'd even celebrated his wedding there. Before the war, this elegant house had been the seat of power in Motakwa County for decades. Before the whites came, this land had been sacred to the Motakwa Indians, who made their last stand on the spot in 1838. And before the natives, some mysterious force had dwelled here since time primeval, pulsing invisibly amidst the frogs and the snakes. Vanderman treasured this history. He learned much of it from the house directly. Ever since he'd spliced his being to Darrow House, the place had whispered in his mind, telling him its secrets.

Fred had many happy memories here, both his own and those of his viciously aristocratic forebears. When he needed a murder to refresh his own powers and recenter himself in the universe, the secluded plantation was his chosen hunting ground. The Knight of the Pure Blood decided he needed to reinforce his magic, especially if he was facing a wizard's war.

Fred found a girl at the truck stop. Finding girls was the easy part. She was young, dark-skinned, with a reddish tint to her hair and big soft eyes. When Fred smelled her, he knew in an instant that she was a distant relation. Her ancestors had lived and died at Darrow House alongside his own. *So much the better,* he thought. *It'll make her a more appealing sacrifice.* Fred reached into the girl's mind, knotting around her memories so that she would perceive him as a trusty and high-tipping regular, even though they'd never seen each other before and he never tipped on principle.

Just as his prey was getting into his car, a vision from the past fell upon the Knight of the Pure Blood. He saw the sights, smelled the odors, felt the hot damp air of days gone by.

Thomas Darrow runs into the night, a saber in one hand and a cavalry pistol in the other. Screams and shouting carry on the wind, together with smoke and falling embers. The fields are on fire. The whole Earth seems on fire. "It's an uprising!" a frightened overseer yells.

Fred gasped in shock. Darrow House was in danger. He peeled off at high speed, leaving the confused girl behind, recklessly blowing through Motakwa County's few stop signs and traffic lights. He tried to telepathically communicate with his lodge brothers, but with the house screaming into his thoughts he couldn't concentrate to send a message.

Winston Darrow peers darkly out the window of his grandly appointed study. A slave runs in, cheerfully announcing that Union troops have taken the rail station. Winston Darrow nods gravely and dismisses the messenger, then slides his grandfather's cavalry pistol into his own mouth and blows his brains out all over the oak paneling.

Turning into the woods, Fred swerved to avoid a tree. He broke into a sweat even though the night was uncommonly cool. A few days ago Fred had thought the idea of stationing deputies at Darrow House was absurd—*the house will do worse to them than Arlen's boys ever could,* he'd argued—but now he wished he'd stationed an army. As he approached the gravel parking lot he saw two empty squad cars, abandoned in the night. Fred skidded to a halt and ran for the big house as fast as he could. The trees by the creek thrashed their limbs about wildly although there was no wind. The dark, rich earth beneath the plantation trembled. Darrow House was panicking.

The storied halls of Darrow House reek of sage and gasoline. Witches in masks and black hoodies dance in the grand ballroom, splashing accelerants even as they conduct an exorcism. The harrowed shade of Winston Darrow appears and lunges for the arsonists, but spectral talons seize him and carry him off into nothingness.

"No!" Fred shrieked. "Oh God, no!"

Darrow House burst into flames, its windows exploding in the eruption of a carefully planned backdraft and sending flickering shards of light flying through the air. Timbers screamed like breaking bones. Centuries of heritage turned to heat and smoke via the simplest of alchemy.

Fred Vanderman glimpsed a sobbing Martha Darrow roasting in her *Gone With The Wind* cotillion finery just as his own body erupted into flame. His intestines boiled in their linings and he could not scream or even breathe due to the pink steam forcing its way out of his lungs. The Knight of the Pure Blood made for the creek in an agonized hobble, frying in his own fat, his flesh blistering and bubbling and sloughing off with each step. He collapsed at the edge of the water and died crawling through the mud.

THE VANDERMAN FUNERAL was a pitiful closed-casket affair. Attendance was poor, since barbarians had recently murdered the sheriff in his own living room and burned the school board president alive. That very afternoon, the FBI announced that it was joining the state police investigation into the killings. The FBI was a willful and mighty spirit, which only the most advanced magicians could command. If it dredged the creek at Darrow House, it might pull up any number of skeletons literal and figurative. When Eli Cawbridge closed his eyes, skeletons came rising up out of the darkness.

RAYMOND LEE SCHULTZE was no history buff like the late Fred Vanderman, and the tombstones of the Long Pines Confederate Cemetery—his own place of power—whispered no secrets in his ears. They only made him angry. The hatred of the men buried here had seeped deep into the ground, coalescing into a bubbling crude that powered the Neo-Nazi sorcerer and all his pagan works.

Notwithstanding Eli's advice to ambush the enemy, Raymond Lee had no patience for hunting in a blind. He spent his days tearing the county apart in search of his foes while his most trusted men stood guard at the cemetery. But he visited nightly to check in and walk the perimeter, and one dark and starry evening, getting out of his truck, he spotted a ghostly light shining amidst the graves.

A commemorative granite monument honoring the Confederacy stood at the center of the cemetery. A fresh, perfectly formed turd sat atop this sacred pedestal. On top of the turd was a severed human hand encrusted in wax, its middle finger outstretched defiantly, and a wick threaded into the fingernail. This gruesome candle gave off a pale, unwholesome light that cast stark shadows across the graveyard. Raymond Lee recognized the charm immediately. It was a Hand of Glory, a hanged man's hand, made into a candle that paralyzed anyone caught in its light. He'd used one to escape from prison in Arkansas, and a runic tattoo on his chest protected him from the effect. Raymond Lee's men, however, were not so shielded. Three of them stood trapped in the radiance, frozen in place like living statues. Only their eyes still moved, flickering back and forth and rolling in helpless terror. Their gazes fixed on Raymond Lee.

Kill them all, whispered an unfamiliar voice, feminine and husky. *They're worthless and they've failed you and you need to kill them all.* If anger was the oil that powered Raymond Lee, now he faced his own Deep-water Horizon, the blowout of a vast underground reserve.

Shrieking obscenities so hard that he spat blood, Raymond Lee punched one of his oldest friends square in the face, smashing the man's nose and toppling him onto his back like an unbalanced mannequin. Raymond Lee pried a tombstone up from the ground and brought it down hard across the fallen man's throat. A stony *crunch* rang out across the cemetery, followed immediately by a wet, croaking death rattle.

The paralyzed Nazis' eyes lit up in terror. They twitched, but could not flee as long as the candle burned.

"You worthless cocksuckers!" Raymond Lee bellowed. "You faggots let some Commie cunt shit all over us!" Raymond Lee picked out another skinhead and methodically pummeled him, singling out the kidneys and the groin for merciless punches. His victim could not even scream, let alone defend himself, and nothing provoked the Knight of the Sword to fury more than a helpless victim, so he chewed off the man's nose and ears as well. He tried to bite off some fingers but the cartilage was too tough to gnaw through. On some level Raymond Lee knew that his mind was being tampered with. However, he was too far gone to care. He sank his teeth into his follower's neck and tore out the jugular. A gusher of salt and copper and heat burst directly into the Knight of the Sword's face. The candle had caught the dying man so completely that he couldn't even fall down, although he was certainly still conscious.

Even under hostile telepathic influence Raymond Lee liked his brutality at a leisurely pace, and while he was killing the skinhead the Hand of Glory's wick sputtered out, plunging the cemetery back into near-total darkness. The skinhead's corpse collapsed with a wet *thwump* and the last survivor—a new kid who'd just been jumped in a week ago at this very spot—let out a heart-rending wail that had been trapped in his throat for the last twenty minutes.

Raymond Lee pounced towards the cry. The graveyard lit up in a strobe of muzzle flashes as the panicked youngster emptied a 9mm magazine at the blood-soaked killer. The charms that had once

protected the Knight of the Sword from harm failed with the cemetery's magic disrupted, and by sheer chance a bullet caught Raymond
Lee in the temple.

The sorcerer died immediately when all the hate that sustained
him squirted out an exit wound in the back of his head. It flowed out
of him in a dark river, pooling at the base of a defiled monument to a
lost cause.

ELI CAWBRIDGE WITNESSED Raymond Lee Schultze's death in a
dream and awoke the same instant that the lodge was reduced to one
member. When he got out of bed he found that he was shaking, and
he hated himself for his weakness at this moment of trial. He decided
that he needed to visit his klavern. Escape was quite impossible. He
knew that he would single-handedly hold Motakwa County, or else he
would perish.

In the basement beneath Eli's church, a door that had always been
locked swung open. The Knight of the Sword's weapons were broken.
The Knight of the Pure Blood's paintings and photos were all torn
down. The Knight of the Threshold's map was defaced. And the
Knight of the Banner's precious flags lay in a smouldering heap of ash
and piss. The enemy had painted their own words of power all over
the walls, their own spells and slogans and the names of their martyrs.
Eli sank to his knees, too shocked to stand.

The witches came out of the corners of the room, twisting time
and space to make their entrance. They carried sharp instruments,
kitchen knives and scissors and hatchets, and wore dark clothing.
There were many of them, Black and White and Asian and Hispanic,
some old, and some young. They were men and women alike, and
others whose genders were as incomprehensible to Eli Cawbridge as
their magic. Some were strangers, some were misfits, and some were
regulars from the pews of the Redeemer's Baptist Church. For all his
paranoia, Eli had never imagined he had so many enemies in his own
hometown, or that such disparate characters might unify against him.

For his lodge to be destroyed by a coven such as this surprised him as badly as if they were undone by a den of raccoons.

In desperation, the Knight of the Banner invoked the mightiest daemon in his grimoire. "I pledge allegiance to the Flag of the United States of America, and to the Republic for which it stands!" he cried. "One nation, under God, with liberty and justice for all!"

Some of the witches chortled. A chill ran down Eli's spine. He hated the sound of women's laughter more than almost anything. One of the witches came up to him and laid a hand on his shoulder. She was clad in tight, head-to-toe black that made her look like a walking shadow, even her eyes hidden behind dark goggles. "Idolatry won't save you now," she said, not unkindly.

"You filth want Motakwa County?" Eli snarled, snapping up to his feet as if he was ready for a fistfight. "You think you can do a better job than the White Lodge?"

"Hard to do worse," the shadow-witch said. "You brought this on yourself, Eli. If you put evil into the universe that's what you'll get back. Power creates resistance—the monolith casts a shadow. It's elementary magic. Your lodge's crimes summoned our coven into being, and you should never summon up what you cannot control." She motioned to her comrades, who circled around.

Eli tried to sing Dixie, but the words stuck in his throat. The coven closed in on him, their weapons flashing, and cut the Knight of the Banner to shreds.

At dawn the police found Eli Cawbridge IV dangling by a noose from the old, crooked oak on Billing Road, clad in his hood and robes, and dripping blood into the roots of the hanging tree.

County law enforcement, still reeling from the death of Sheriff Clemmer and a slate of outside investigations, never closed the preacher's killing, or that of Fred Vanderman, or even that of Sheriff Clemmer himself, although they did catch the kid who shot Raymond Lee. But people had gotten accustomed to unsolved killings over the years, and in due time life moved along. A new sheriff was elected, the first Black sheriff in the county's history. A cheerful young preacher took over at Redeemer's Baptist Church. His first sermon was on the theme of fresh beginnings.

The old, crooked oak tree on Billing Road died suddenly the next year, even though the plants around it were thriving. That summer, sweet-smelling flowers bloomed in vast abundance across Motakwa County, and cool breezes brought relief from the stifling heat.

THE PIG-MEN'S MUD MOTEL
BY PATRICK BARB

After the City Council and the Golden Boy Mayor passed those weak-ass reforms, the Pig-Men seized all land on the other side of the tracks, setting up a mini police-state.

Trash can fires directly from '80s side-scrolling video games burn all night. Rivers of piss and piles of shit—all courtesy of the Pig-Men—mark the border. The stench hits you from miles away.

When they catch an outsider approaching the blockade, they shout random criminal citations, like Pentecostal preachers speaking in tongues. Accuse folks of littering. Trespassing. No trial follows. Just a bullet or twenty in the cranium of an offender before the unlucky bastard even asks, "What the actual fuck?"

Sick Nick's lucky. And that's the first and last time I'll say it.

The Pig-Men patrol we encounter lights him the fuck up. Then, move on right after, leaving his body where it falls. He'll get nibbled and gnawed on by rats, pigeons, and the occasional tweaking raccoon.

(I doubt Nicky felt anything besides relief when they aerated him via a roaring chorus of AR-15s. The dude's got enough malignant tumors for a pick-up basketball game. *Every life's sacred? Nah, sometimes death is sacred as fuck.*)

Though, when I think about it, maybe Nicky would've liked the Hog Pen.

The stories passed around describe massive sows and boars wallowing in mud and cigarette ash, eyes bloodshot, receiving evening blessings in Keystone Light and Wild Turkey.

Good way to get rid of bodies as they say in the movies. Train 'em toward an appetite for annihilation. From what we've heard, the all-human diet gets 'em stretched out. Makes the skin roomy enough for a man to fit inside.

On the border, a Mama possum and her mewling offspring chow on Nick's cancerous lung tissue. Mama hisses when we get the animal control pole's steel cable loop around the dead man's foot and cinch tight. No time to apologize. We drag Nick back into the dark on our side of town.

"We're at the spot."

"Huh?"

Deena came from Portland about a month ago. The whole West Coast's uninhabitable, with the perpetual wildfires, sinkholes, and whatever other Biblical shit's thrown at 'em. We're taking on as many climate refugees as possible or steering folks away from the Pig-Men, at a minimum.

Last reports from our fire-roasted comrades indicated Deena put in good work during the SoCal Earthquake Riots. The L.A. Sheriff Gangs drove their tank gulags through studio lots and served as predecessors to the Pig-Men's takeover.

So, I'm surprised how often Deena's slow on the uptake, oblivious to what's going on.

But, hey, education's power, right?

"They left Nicky and moved on…"

Another long pause.

"Means it's safe enough to cross."

Deena nods like a kindergartner marveling at a backward recitation of the ABCs. Her eyes move slower than I'd expect, before drifting to the barricade and dear departed Nicky. "What about him?"

"Someone'll collect him."

But there's one more thing to do.

I pull out an industrial stapler and secure the crinkled sheet of notebook paper pulled from my back jeans pocket onto Nick's face. "No coffin, please. Just wet, wet mud." The strict instructions left for his body's disposal will double as the funeral shroud.

"See ya in Hell, bud."

"C'mon," I say to Deena, putting the stapler in my go-bag and pulling out my butcher's knife. It's a giant oversized novelty gift taken from a fancy-ass charcuterie. But sharp enough to cut you, if you so much as look at it the wrong way.

When I step on the tracks, the tread of my boot fills with the steaming shit of a stray turd. Deena follows me into the Pig-Men's territory. Their motel's dead ahead.

"I'M SCARED."

I strain to hear my little bro's whispered confession, delivered from his lips through one of the cheap black plastic receivers on the phones at the Lakeside Terrace Motel and onto my burner phone.

(Before anyone asks, there aren't lakes near the Lakeside Terrace Motel, unless you count unpaved sinkholes.)

We're protesting the new police reform outside City Hall. Once again, nobody's willing to go far enough. They stick us with another round of ridiculous centrist, back-patting bending over backward to ensure piss-scared suburban voters "cops are our friends, *honest.*"

They believe forcing these jack-boot bullies into the neighborhoods they've run roughshod over for years will change things!

Standing shoulder to shoulder with placard-wielding Resistance Moms and more mean bastards like myself, something's missing.

The realization hits hard. There isn't a single Nazi skinhead instigating piece of shit in attendance. No lipless survivalists clad in Confederate Flag body armor, no trust-fund wannabe ubermensch in flipped-up collar, pink Polos filming footage to "own the libs."

And, no cops.

Flanked by his staff, the Mayor stumbles on the white limestone steps of City Hall. No escort and none of the J. Crew rejects surrounding him appear qualified for a Presidential physical fitness medal let alone running private security detail.

My phone rings once. Then stops. Then two more rings. Stops. Three more and … I know my baby brother Ricky's calling, using a signal we developed.

On the steps, the Mayor's microphone whines and screeches behind a podium. I cup my hand over the ear I'm not holding my phone to, isolating the sound of my brother's sobs.

"Where are you?"

He tells me he checked in at the Lakeside for the night. My first instinct's to ask how much money he needs. When it comes to sex work, Ricky's a dabbler, treating it like driving an Uber for a weekend but sweatier. But he likes the work and the clients. Location aside, the kid oozes safety from every pore.

Some of the ladies working at the same motel act as big sisters or cool aunts. They watch out for him, letting Ricky bum cigarettes or use the toilet in one of their rented-by-the-hour rooms because one of his johns clogged up *his* commode with cum rags. (True story.)

"Ladies and gen'lemen, effective this afternoon, the city police and police departments of our surrounding metropolitan area resigned en masse from their contracts." The Mayor's slurring his words like he's funneling Jack Daniels. The way his aides wrinkle their noses, maybe I'm not far off target…

"The pigs are coming!" Ricky's exclamation pulls me back to our conversation. There's a fear and panic in his speech, unlike anything I've heard before.

And we've both experienced some shit.

I push through the crowd, figuring without the cops it'll be easier exiting from the front. "Pigs? How can you tell?"

"Some of 'em have their uniforms on. Not all, but also…"

"But cops never mess with Lakeside though."

I leave unspoken the reasons why the cops steer clear of Lakeside —the massive bribes the vice squad takes from the motel's owners, pimps, independent sex workers, and drug dealers, alongside the side hustles of many beat cops who pursue *their* drug-running and pimping extracurriculars there.

I weave through sweaty bodies pressed together with their posterboard signs drooping.

Figures it's kicking off on one of the hottest days of the year. Summertime always brings out bad shit.

Ricky goes quiet and I imagine him wiping away tears and snot bubbles like in childhood. In front of City Hall, media springs up like journalism jack-in-the-boxes wound tight too many times. They come hungry for fresh news meat.

They shout questions at the Mayor and his team like they're declaring war. "Where've the police gone?" "Did all cops resign or *just* the bad apples? All of them? All?" "What'll happen to our neighborhoods?" "Are you willing to accept blame for the inevitable increase in crime?" "Do you not back the blue, sir?"

"They're filling the parking lot. Squad cars. SWAT transports. Tanks. They've even got body armor on the goddamn horses." Ricky's breathless narration sweeps me up, so it's like I'm at the Lakeside with him.

"You're fucking with me…?"

Ricky coughs out a laugh like I'd slammed a fist into his nuts. His *Ha!* fizzles like cigarette ash in a rain puddle.

"There's something else…"

"Yeah?"

The toe of my sneaker touches the lip of City Hall's bottom step.

"They're actual pigs."

"What?"

The Mayor whines and his mic feedback responds in kind. "Excuse me, sir. Excuse me…"

The would-be wunderkind politico stabs his finger in my direction, like there's a magic button he'll press to make me go away. My focus is on Ricky though.

"The cops … they're wearing…"

"Excuse me…"

The Mayor again. I stare daggers into the creep's face. Something about my bald head, thick red beard, neck tattoos, and all-black ensemble gives off a negative impression.

Which is absolutely on purpose.

Ricky whimpers in my ear. It gets my mental wires crossed. Instead of telling off Mr. Mayor, I end up shouting my response to my brother. "All the cops are wearing pig skins?"

Like setting off a row of sparklers, the questions from the journalists and the flashing bulbs of the cameras go off one after the other. I don't need my picture taken, so I make a run for it.

There's a single gunshot, one last desperate sulfuric "pity me," but I'm out of time for turning around.

DAYS LATER, I learn the Mayor pulled out a snubbed-nose revolver and Bud Dwyered himself all over his remaining staff of suck-ups.

I won't speak ill of them any further though. A few of them even work with us in the cooperative. Getting bits of skull and brain on your Oxfords tends to radicalize people.

They've boarded-up houses on the Pig-Men's side of town. From the sketchy reports we'd get from before the Pig-Men raided the electric grid, forcing the workers to turn off the power on their side of town, and then stole generators from the Home Depots, they seized all the houses and apartments, crammed any survivors into the motel. There's this occupying army pissing right on the Third Amendment of their beloved Constitution.

But, like any pig in shit, those assholes only care about Number 2.

Under the cover of shadows and debris, our approach to the Pig-Men's motel puts truth to the rumors. A godawful medley of stenches wafts from the row homes. Like a skunk's spray squirting through splintered gaps in shot-up plywood. I recognize the Pig-Men's signature bouquet from their occasional raiding parties. They don't cross the border our way often. Probably because we've got enough white faces and greenbacks so even those dumbshits worry they'll draw attention of the state or federal variety.

But fucking with the poor and the dispossessed? *That's America, man.*

We catch another sign of the Pig-Men's takeover in the form of piles and piles of roasted bodies left on the street. Each corpse stack's a tangle of charbroiled limbs, impossible to separate man from woman, children from adults. Charcoal black skeletons pile up in gutters along trash-strewn sidewalks, like someone drew the snow-plow through mountains of dead flesh.

Deena's boot crunches the red and green colored glass of a Christmas tree ornament, spreading shards on the crimson-stained concrete. I shake my head. Before I get her attention, there's a shout behind us.

"Halt!"

I've trained for this exact scenario. So, you bet your sweet ass when the shaking, shivering Pig-Man gives his muffled command through some dead hog's bruised snout, I refuse to comply. Instead, I swing the broad surface of the novelty butcher knife over to protect my body's center mass. *Ping ping ping.*

Bullets ricochet off metal. Sparks singe the skin on my knuckles, but I hold on tight. One bullet gets through, grazing my clavicle. Sweater wool, skin, and bone fragment explode against my cheek. Biting through my bottom lip to keep from screaming, I draw more blood.

Still, I keep moving. The blade strikes the top of the spoiled pig's face mask. Its razor-sharp edge splits open the tender, rotting skin until it's bisected and splayed apart revealing a human face. His close-cropped hair's covered in bloody mucus. Here's his second birth in filth and murmured obscenity.

I bring the blade down again, slicing the snout from the pig's head. Another swing and the officer's nose comes off. Now, his mug's a hell of a lot closer to the pig's face he wore. One more slice across his waddling neck and I'm done with him for good.

Deena's got out the industrial meat grinder our gunsmith anarchist comrades modified into a crank-operated machine gun spitting out fat wads of bullets like Peter North on the beaches of Normandy. She swings her hips from side to side, hand tight on the trigger, crank, or whatever you want to call it. I wipe the pig's blood from my eyes and put a hand on her back. Ignoring the lumpy texture beneath her skin, I give a quick squeeze. "Easy."

"What?"

I point to the swirling floodlights ahead of us. When we follow the lights to their source, we'll reach the motel. We'll get to Ricky.

"No one's coming. Bet they figure anyone coming this close to their home base is stupid as hell."

"And we're stupid?" Deena asks.

"Yeah, we're the fucking stupidest."

THE FIRST NIGHT in a world with the Pig-Men is ... a lot. Cable news crews flock to the border, wanting to give the crazies in porcine flesh a chance to explain themselves. Because, of course, they've gotta "both sides" everything. The fresh pig flesh sits tight on their bodies. When their leader—going by "Sarge"—takes center-stage, a chorus of snorting cheers follows.

"We're sick and tired of the disrespect. You wanna call us 'pigs' and try to ruin good men and women with accusations when we work hard every day? Well, we'll show you what real pigs we can be. Pig-Men. Gonna start by doing something about *your* crimes against the truth."

The journalists shout questions, but they're drowned out by chortling hogs. Until the Chief raises a modified hoof-hand for silence. Everyone on our side of town's leaning close to their TVs by this point. Because who wouldn't want a front-row seat for the freak show?

When the Pig-Men open fire on the TV crews, I think it sinks in for the fence-sitters. Here's something beyond a difference of opinion.

Hope it makes it easier to move folks from "Defund the Police" to "Destroy the Police."

But for now, everyone's exhausted. So *fucking* exhausted.

Early the next morning of the second day or late night on the first day (Not sure which, as I blew through enough coke to tell everyone about five separate screenplay ideas—if not for more pressing concerns. And time's meaningless besides.), my phone rings. One ring, then silence.

But I pick up.

"Ricky?"

Gunfire on the line.

Glass breaks.

"Ricky?"

He shushes me. Long, loud, like a sudden burst of static in my ear. So intense, I've gotta hold the phone away from my ear. When I get it back in place, the line's dead.

"Son of a bitch."

Someone's in my bed and they ask, "What the hell happened?"

Or there's no one. But my day's crazy enough, so I pretend I'm *not* talking to myself when I answer.

(They were fucking fantastic whoever they weren't.)

"As kids, when we shared a room, Ricky'd shush me when he got tired of me talking his ear off. It's his way of letting me know he's okay, and it's time for me to sleep."

If anyone is there with me, it sounds like I've bored them into silence.

THE CALLS and the SHHHHHHHHHHHHHs continue for weeks, months. I don't know where Ricky is, except I know he's calling from the motel. I imagine him moving from room to room, hiding out wherever he can. I'm okay if I get his nightly calls.

Then, they stop.

So, I make plans.

A RING OF PATROL CARS, blue and red lights swirling in the night sky like American flag afterbirth, surrounds the motel. Deena watches the lights. Her tight-skinned, too-smooth face goes blue, then red. Red, then blue. She's not listening as I review our plan.

It's okay. This plan's still-born.

A squad of Pig-Men walks the perimeter on teensy black-hooved trotters like they're wearing stiletto heels. The tattered remnants of their pig skin's cock or pussy flap and flutter in the night breeze on some X-rated Porky Pig shit.

I drop down and pull Deena with me, so we're crouching behind a cruiser. Someone's spray-painted over the department motto. "To protect $ and serve the HOG."

"Perceptive shit for the piggies," I whisper.

"Huh?" Deena asks her question loud, like a dog's bark on a street where no dog lives.

She's scratching at her face, too. Going to town.

"Never mind," I say, "Bet some *real* survivors wrote it. Last will and testament shit."

OF COURSE, my people get on board with the plan to save Ricky. We draw up plans to hit 'em hard and fast. With an army matching theirs, minus the fetishistic Nazi-fucker uniforms and death cult mindset. I've got guys, gals, and enby pals, ready to ride.

Until the "Survivors" ruin it. They're the folks who gave themselves the nickname, who change their Facebook profile pics to "raise awareness," and who insisted on patience and bipartisanship in the lead-up to the Pig-Men's rise.

Survivors? Ha!

Not like they're in Ricky's shoes. Not like they're affected in any truly life-threatening manner. *Oh no, you can't get fast food because the staff's getting murdered and tortured by pig flesh-clad cops and cop worshippers? Boo-fucking-hoo.*

Some assholes demand the governor send in the National Guard or go so far as to suggest the President send in troops. But no one in power wants to touch our city with a ten-foot pole. They're afraid of the Pig-Men, thinking in terms of disease, worried it'll spread to other cities, other states. Hell, other countries.

I bet they grow their pigs plenty large in the UK.

They drag out one concession from me. Getting me to strip down the operation.

So, it's me, Sick Nick (who's dying), and the new girl Deena. They say she's perfect for the job.

Yeah, I'm gonna say it…

Almost *too* perfect.

I'm on top of the patrol car. One or two Pig-Men snouts turn my way. Their human eyes straining to find me through the extra layers of flesh. This new religion's a clumsy, burdensome one if anything.

But I don't want the attention of some, I want them all.

I kick the shit out of the car's lights. Steel-toed boots send shards skittering across the asphalt of the parking lot. It does the trick.

"Freeze!"

They've got their service weapons taped to their swollen hoofs, so they don't have to draw. In seconds, I'm covered. One of them, an early adopter of the Pig-Men lifestyle, considering his pig skin's gray, like spoiled meat, with a coating of flies doubling as a goatee, tilts his head toward a tiny black radio unit clipped to his shirt front. The effort gives his piggy face a triple chin, smooshing his malleable, rotting snout.

Time's running out. I turn around and throw my butcher's knife. Right into Deena's forehead.

Bullseye.

Gotta move fast. I shrug off my black hoodie, exposing my pale skin to the poisoned night air. Making sure everyone notices the C4 strapped to my chest, stomach, and back.

Don't worry, I didn't kill Deena. The butcher's blade hits the perfect spot, splitting the seams on the Deena-face. Probably skinned alive to keep the skin malleable enough to make a mask from it. Poor long-dead Deena's preserved skin cracks like the shell of an old baseball. A man's pale white face emerges. Wearing a dead woman's hands, he touches his exposed cheeks.

"Howdy, officer," I say, with an exaggerated wave.

I don't get to say more. One of the Pig-Men gets smart, scrambling up on the hood of the car, close enough to reach me. A baton strikes the back of my legs, and I crumble. Someone shouts a warning. "Don't let him fall with all those bombs."

Squishy, befouled hands, greasy with stranger danger, pull me from the car. Hog limbs wrap anaconda-tight around my neck, squeezing. First, stars.

Then, black.

APPROACHING the checkpoint into Pig-Men territory, Sick Nick pulls me back and we let Deena take the lead. She keeps walking because it's the last thing we told her to do. And she's sure damn good at following orders.

"You know they're a cop, right?"

"Deena from out west?"

Nicky's head shakes. "Naw, man. Me and my tumors hear things, man. People whispering to the Pig-Men when they think no one's around. That's how we know they ain't Deena from out west. Whoever they are."

I pull him close. "Who *is* it?"

"A cop."

Something about the way he says it, the certainty there, I've gotta believe him. My mind races, thinking about the Pig-Men and how hard it might get for them to find pigs big enough to wear. *Wouldn't it be so much easier to find someone else's skin to wear? So much easier for a cop with a bad rap—maybe a few officer-related shootings on his record, say—to hide out in some antifascist punk's skin…*

OF COURSE, they set the Hog Pen up in the lobby of the motel. The ooze stretches across the reception area and out the shattered glass front to where the drop-off loop used to be. Monster sows and hogs buried up to their snouts in primordial muck, squeals like crying babies. When I come to, the first thing I'm wondering is, *Why haven't they killed me?*

Sarge—pig-faced commander of the monster sect—stands before me, in a dress uniform covered in medals and ribbons, like he's play-acting as a war hero.

So, they're making an example of me.

There's Ricky, bone-skinny and cuffed to one of Sarge's hoofs. Eyes rolled back white, so I can't tell if my baby brother's even alive. The killer cop, the one I recognize from the news, the one who wore Deena's skin, steps forward. He kneels before Sarge.

Then he strips away the rest of the dead woman's skin. Sarge grunts and more Pig-Men step forward, carrying the stretched-out, freshly-removed skin of another pig. They drape it over Not-Deena's naked form, covering his semi-hard cock until it presses against the dead hog's abdomen.

A staple gun explodes across the pig's belly and chest, sealing away the man.

The Pig-Man's time has come. He picks up the C4 and drapes it across his shoulders like a prayer shawl.

I'm gonna die here.

"Hey, Ricky!" I shout, trying to pull him back from whatever abyss the Pig-Men's torture has brought him to the brink of.

No answer. The Pig-Men snort and snuff, stomping and splashing in the mud with the pigs from which they take their flesh.

"Ricky!"

Nothing.

Sarge and the new Pig-Man (who's not Deena) laugh, heads back like mustache-twirling villains in a Saturday morning cartoon.

"Nice white skin on a big hoss sunuvabitch. You coulda been one of *us*."

Sarge doesn't matter. None of them matter.

"Ricky!"

Shhhhhhhhhh. Lips cracked and powdery white, the shushing sound carries the death-rattle.

My baby brother's got something more infectious than the Pig-men. He's got a hell of a smile. I've gotta smile too.

Makes sense.

On those late nights when we shared a room, whenever I'd stop talking and we listened to the shouting and the crying and the promises for a better tomorrow, we'd take a blood oath, swearing to die smiling if we got to die together.

Ricky gets us started. With his free hand, he grabs for the chain connecting him to the Pig-Men's Führer. He takes off running. Pulling hard. Doing the best his wasted-away limbs can manage.

Surprise is on our side. Ricky takes Sarge off his trotters, dragging his greasy bacon-fat across the tiny strip of tile flooring they've kept dry. Mud and shit splash up from the hellish pit, covering everyone nearby. Even I'm wiping wormy shit from my eyes and lips. And I'm laughing. Ricky pulls the bastard down into the Hog Pen.

Then the real pigs come to feed.

Blood oozes up. A deep red stain spreads across the gray surface.

All around me, something breaks in the beady black eyes of the Pig-Men. Men, women, white, black, Latinx, Hispanic, the good apples, and the bad. Tears stream down bristly snouts.

It's my brother who died. What the fuck do they have to be sad about?

Then, a hoof emerges from the waste. From the blood and mud, Pig-Man Sarge drags himself back to drier land. Chunks of second skin hang loose and bloodless. Still wearing my C4, the Not-Deena Pig-Man embraces his commander. Sarge "blesses" him with a vomit cocktail straight from his snout to the others. He luxuriates in this unholy blessing. Writhing in a painful sort of ecstasy.

I can't make myself process what I'm watching though. I'm a voyeur on the surface. And underneath, I miss my brother.

All I can think about it is how Ricky might've done things differently. Hadn't the ladies working at the Lakeside showed him how to get out of handcuffs? Hadn't they showed how to hold his breath for the particularly unhygienic clients? Hadn't one of them even demonstrated how to keep a big fucking razor under your tongue?

Hadn't they…

Sarge stomps across to where I'm standing. Using his free hoof, he waves away the other Pig-Men surrounding me. "I hope you're happy, you bastard."

If I could work up any saliva, I'd hock a loogie in his piggy face.

But his eyes aren't how I remembered. No beady, black. They're green, like emeralds. "Ric…"

Shhhhhhhhhhh.

"I'm okay. Now, you can sleep."

THE CHAD SHOW
BY ANA E. ROBIC

Eleven minutes into his nightly broadcast, Chad Spears straightens his royal blue necktie and looks right into the camera.

"But enough talk about the legislative details. Enough talk about subcommittees and hearings. Let's cut to what's really at stake here," he says to 25 million American viewers. "I've seen what leftists want. It doesn't matter which group of them you're talking about, whether it's the academic elite or the laziest welfare leeches. What they want—liberals, democrats, antifa, heathens, homosexuals—is to destroy our Western values." He gestures gravely to the jumbo American flag mounted by his desk.

A bead of sweat forms on his brow. The camera crew gives him a thumbs-up and a smile. Kathy with the clipboard sagely nods.

"Now what does that mean, 'destroy our Western values'?" Chad asks, narrowing his eyes. "It's not just about raising your taxes or teaching your children that it's shameful to be white. That's part of it, for sure, but it goes deeper, and darker. It means undoing—at every level—tradition, freedom, hard work, and sacrifice. It means spitting in the face of basic personal responsibility, of earning your keep. Listen up, I'm gonna tell you an ugly truth: leftists want to do away with folks like you and me. Not just our values, but us. That's right. And I can show you. They want a world without faithful Christians. They want to end the American family. They want to emasculate the American man."

Chad's voice gets loose and excited. "Did that get your attention? Oh you betcha they do. These perverts are obsessed with taking down the so-called patriarchy. They are obsessed with insulting the manhood of our fathers, with the potency of men like me."

Standing up from behind the broadcast desk, Chad looks fearlessly forward like a saint at the gallows.

"Fellow Americans, THIS is what the left wants!"

He punches himself in the groin. A pause. Then again. And again. First gently, but soon furiously. Tears and low-pressure vomit leak from his face as he screams nonwords, doubling over. But the punching does not stop.

WHACK right in the crotch. The sound is like a sopping bath towel dropped on tile.

SQUARP directly to his tender ailing gonads.

Far away, a General Motors marketing executive calls the network to double their advertising. Tonight he will dream of gleefully slaughtering cows filled with ten-dollar bills.

Chad Spears keeps striking himself mercilessly between the legs with his bare hand. Sobbing, he calls out, "This is what antifa will do to you! To you! Oh God my pelvis—why?!" The crew has wheeled and tilted their cameras so that even on the gray carpeted floor, he is elegantly and professionally centered.

Chad's fist will not be dissuaded. Millions at home in front of their 4K televisions watch, and as if speaking with one giant mouthwatering grin, they hiss, "Yesssss," unaware of each other. Behold a shared wonder, a shimmer of real civilian unity.

With his right hand, the sobbing anchorman reaches up to his desk and grabs a coffee mug emblazoned with "YOUR MOTHER WAS PRO-LIFE"—a new weapon with which to ravage his body. His left hand, meanwhile, rends his clothing in clumsy panic.

BAM with the mug, this time to his face. A red oozing starts at the hairline, slow and coagulated. "Liberals! Democrats! OH JESUS. Leftism is doing this to you, ladies and gentlemen!"

CRACK the mug shatters into big chunks on the bridge of Chad's nose, breaking skin and bone. An involuntary wet sound poots out of his mouth like a walrus farting at SeaWorld. Grasping the broken mug by its handle, he drags a sharp edge down his face and into his soft white chest, ripping all along the way, his chest ready and waiting to be opened like an Amazon Prime delivery box. Then comes a frantic flapping noise and a mass of pink gristle shoots from his belly, landing somewhere.

From behind a glass balcony, the show's executive producer whispers, "This is incredible. His best show yet. This is our Pulitzer." She looks around and yells, "Can someone make sure Mr. Walton is seeing this?"

"Gaaawwwwaaa," gurgles the mangy fiend on live TV. For a moment he stares point blank at his wedding ring, and then in a single terrible move bites off the finger at its second knuckle. It's not easy to tell where it went.

He drags himself to the base of the American flag and looks up at its tricolor fabric in truckling reverence. Right fist clenched around porcelain shards, he drives home another whack to his genitalia. Liquid of every sort begins streaming in thick washes. The man's body writhes and he mumbles, "Antifa."

"Keep going!" pleads Kathy with the clipboard from behind the crew. She smiles widely and nods like a puppy trainer.

Chad is clawing at himself now with the directionless fury of an ant colony under boiling water, gripping and tearing any chunk he can leverage. Each convulsion broadcasts anatomical fragilities hitherto unknown: a nipple twists off with trivial effort, clumps of scalp rip out when enough hair is pulled, and ear cavities are, in fact, fully thumb-deep. Yes.

Up comes Chad's massacred left hand, and—WRATCH—lips are yanked free and squeezed like a sponge, leaving his mouth spewing in borderless pain and shrieking grotesquery. With no human purpose left, the orifice takes to chewing its tongue out. Because Chad is now forever unable to speak, the production team has typed flashing text into the chyron. "THIS IS WHAT LEFTISTS ARE DOING TO YOU RIGHT NOW!" explains the network in helpful Times New Roman.

Chad is losing consciousness but his rhythmic mutilation continues, having accrued a life of its own. With each broad swing of his arms, his torso splits wider.

"It sounds like peeling duct tape, doesn't it?" whispers a cameraman. He zooms in on the bone peeking, becoming visible. "The sternum, they call it," he mumbles to nobody, remembering ninth-grade biology class..

Saltwater tears gush, and a shredded digestive tract opens up from within, inverting the esophagus and pushing it inch by inch slowly from the mouth through which Chad that morning had eaten Jimmy Dean sausage. Indeed, impossible things are now happening to his body. America watches in childlike jouissance as novel colors of vomit overtake his familiar features. Nothing will be the same.

Like a careless archeologist, the star of *The Chad Show* excavates himself greedily, stratum after stratum. A pancreas throbs disconnected on the floor. Fox News will definitely have to replace this carpet. In the meantime, they have begun playing John Mayer's "Your Body Is a Wonderland" atop the ordeal. Absolutely everyone likes this song. Even still, viewers can hear a new sound erupting from the tattered ghoul: "WOOWWWWWW!"

Yes. The moment of WOW has arrived. It is a noise of pure wonder, a creature's utterance in mid-discovery of entirely new experiential qualia. All speech apparatus ruined, WOW is the only sound still available to this writhing gutmass. And yet it is singularly expressive and wholly sufficient.

"WOW!" it howls with alien delight, its mouth awkwardly full of cartilage tubing. A fistful of useless scrotal remains are tossed at the camera. They splat, and 50 million American eyes fixate on a ruptured left testicle, its salmon-colored goo dripping down the lens.

"WOOWW!" A new octave is revealed. Everyone agrees it is a beautiful day. The price of Bitcoin skyrockets.

The thing that was Chad somehow yanks an entire femur from its thigh, and imbued with the divine strength of WOW, splits the bone in half. Like Paula Deen dressing a Cobb salad, the animal drizzles itself in thin marrow. With a single gesture, the broken halves of the bone are then plunged deep into the eyeballs. They jut from the sockets like pacifiers protruding from babies.

As if stirred to carnal impulse, the abomination's hips start gyrating. Yes. Everyone's hips start gyrating—everyone in the studio, everyone watching TV, everyone driving a Chevrolet. "WOW," they whisper in cosmic unison. This erotically unholy splatter is the work, surely, of degenerate progressives, transsexual globalists, twerking environmentalists. This engorged frenzy of suffering is what tolerance begets. It is what socialist professors are teaching the young. It is what will happen if we defund the police. Oh God yes. All of it.

And then in one cataclysmic explosion, the thing flexes the large intestine, bursting in all directions the black and purple digestia within. An eruption of visceral magma. A Versailles fountain of fecal gore. The lethally transcendent orgasm of all right-thinking churchgoers, made manifest in that last pelvic holocaust.

"WOOWWWWWW!" One final reverberant cry. One more sorrowful song. The odd punctuating squish emanating from no identifiable cause.

It takes a few minutes for America to catch its breath. The John Mayer tune is over. The camera swivels past the colon-soaked flag and settles its gaze on the innocuous wooden door at the set's edge. After a little silence, Kathy with the clipboard barks, "Cue the next one!"

The door opens and a handsome thirty-something man with severe eyebrows steps out, carefully over the worthless guts. He looks into the camera, its lens still runny with blood and lukewarm semen. "This has been Chad Spears," he smiles, adjusting his royal blue necktie. "Tune in to *The Chad Show* tomorrow night to find out more of the terrors that leftism has in store for you. Till then, America, stay safe."

Dear Santa,

It is me Tatum on December 1 and I have been good this year. On a scale of one to 10 its 8. What I want most for Christmas is a Chad Show Action Set please. Sometimes you bring candy and clothes but this year a Chad Show Action Set is all I need. Mom and Dad say it is polite to tell why a present is importent so you dont look greedy. So here is what it has.

1 real Chad eyebrows which matters so I can look like him. He is a great American and we need more.

2 Chad goo so I can bleed a lot but there is also a pump you can put under your arm to make it spray everywhere. That is what librals want is to make us bleed and so the goo is how you show it. The goo washes off.

3 organs and this is special because when you lose your lunges and kidney ect. it shows how leftism is taking apart my family

4 a Chad Strap which is a cup like you wear for soccer. It sounds really gross I know but its the most importent part of the Chad Show Action set. In the ad a guy hits himself so many times because of black lives matter. When I grow up I will be a real Chad and it wont be fake. A kid on tiktok did it without a Chad Strap and he almost died.

5 a blue tie its just part of the costume but it helps and blue is the nicest color, I like every shade of it.

6 a John Mayer CD o.k. I dont have a CD player but there is one in the jeep and I like to hear him sing your body is a wonder land. Some times I pretend it is me who the song is about.

If you get extra packs you can also get bonus organs like the Leaping Liver and a Chad bone which is your leg bone but I dont need those. Not yet ha ha ha! One thing is that my Dad wants a shirt he saw on the show that says ANTI-ANTIFA. It would be cool if I had one too so we match.

Mom says I need to ask for books to read too so anything about how to scream louder is good. Its very funny when I go WOWWWWWW I even do it in church.

Thanks and merry Christmas
Connor
PS bitcoin

SNORTING GHOSTS IN THE CAUSE
OF ANTI-FASCISM

BY CAIAS WARD

Ever punch someone so hard they pass through the Wall Between Worlds and end up on the side where all the ghosts are?

This is not an idle question, but an important one, and me showing off, because this afternoon *I punched someone so hard they passed through the Wall Between Worlds and ended up on the side with all the ghosts.*

Anyway, I got separated from my friends at the protest when the cops tried to kettle us. I took the chance to swap out of my black bloc clothing on the quick and see who I could blend in with so I could get out of the area. I met Cheryl and Kenny, bunch of old-school punks in their early fifties who had settled down after the rough and rowdy '90s to raise kids in the suburbs. They still were in shape, still flew the flag, ink all over they weren't ashamed of showing, Gripfasts instead of Docs, but they looked like that one friend's mom and dad who were the 'cool' ones. I liked them, a lot. Cheryl was a librarian at a local uni, kind of witchy in a way you can be when you have tenure. Kenny was a union plumber, thick wrists with sleeves showing where he stood when it came to racists. I didn't tell them my real name, said I was Steve, because of OpSec, just like I had left my phone at home. For all they knew, I was Just Another Student in the Area.

We talked about bands and shows and they saw Rollins and they saw Bad Brains and lots of other bands I wish I could have seen in their prime. Cheryl and Kenny were the old guard, back in the bad old days when skinheads would hang out somewhere and if you didn't fumigate, your bar or arcade became a skinhead hive and no one else could show up without getting harmed. They both had the scars, serious ones from brawls, talking about them like they were showing off their kids (Hank, 26 and a lawyer; Debbie, 21, Princeton). It was a strange vibe from them, as if Patti Smith and Mick Jones showed up at your door to welcome you to the neighborhood.

And then Cheryl and Kenny and I ended up face to face with four guys in polo shirts and tight-sided haircuts while we were cutting through a parking deck to duck even more cops trying to kettle black bloc and locals. Lots of thoughts ran through me, like *were they deliberately leading me off to their friends?* and *are we gonna get our asses kicked?* I have no idea why I broke my own rules: stay with your people, don't go off alone. I felt like I could trust these two, and now their friends were going to—

No, these weren't their friends. I knew this because Kenny picked up one of those metal garbage cans, the big heavy ones they put in places so they don't get knocked around, and threw it at the crowd. Kenny caught one of them in the leg, the tight-haired fascie ragdolling on top of the can and rolling off. The guy, short and chunky and clearly the pinnacle of masculinity, scraped and screamed on the ground, his arm slick with blood. His friends didn't know what to do at first, especially when Cheryl and Kenny took out little baggies from their pockets. The dust inside was translucent, wispy glitter which stretched and moaned when they put a bit on their fingers and snorted.

"Snort up, baby, we have work to do," Cheryl said in a way which meant 'you are my kid' or 'you are going to have a threesome with us', I wasn't sure. She cupped her hand over my mouth and nose, poking me in the back. I breathed in on reflex, the gooey dust in her hand clawing through my nose and the color washing out of my vision. It climbed through my sinuses, gripping and ripping and screaming at me.

The world was grey and decayed, every hint of wear and want and gloom magnified. The polo-shirted chuds, once fleshy and pink, were now marked with age and collapse. Even the one's blood slick on his arm was not red, but deep and dark and void. It whispered at me with each pulse of his heart, encouraging me to accept the end of all things and—

"Don't listen to the voices. Just throw hands," Kenny said, his grip on my shoulder. I turned to him, his face cragged and gaunt, the inevitability of death scrawled on his skin. I shook my head, blinking to clean my eyes, and seeing nothing but death painted on every surface. Cheryl's kind face was now hooked and hagged, Baba Yaga in Mom jeans. She laughed at the terror rushing through me, clucking her tongue.

"Baby, guess you've never snorted ghosts before," Cheryl said.

Kenny was already balls-deep in the crowd, his own personal mosh pit. He threw hands and feet, laughing at their punches, then silent as the four men swarmed him. Cheryl jumped on, peeling and pulling away at them, punches to kidneys and kicks to legs. She ate a backhand, the blood on her mouth dark and calling me before she spit it back at her attacker. One of the chuds broke free from the gang-pile on Kenny, swinging on Cheryl with his flabby arms. She ducked and moved, teasing and taunting him, pulling him away, shooting a look at me.

Now, I've been to a few protests and it's not like I haven't punched people before. Hell, I once kicked some racist fuck in the ribs until their skin split. I knew one thing; the only part of a 'sucker-punch' is the sucker getting hit. I lined up and put my fist square in his neck, hard knuckles into soft throat.

The air ripped around the guy, like I was shoving him underwater. He splashed though whatever barrier it was, his skin scraping through the howling hooks and barbs as it opened up. As quick as it opened, the barrier closed with the barest ripple, cutting off the screams from the other side as I yanked my hand away from the snapping maw. The flabby man, more a boy than anything, skidded on the floor of the parking deck as though it were snow, a slushy detritus like what I snorted covering everything. He tried to stand, struggling in the ethereal muck. He was translucent now, and confused, staring through his own limbs and the washed out blood from the many rips and tears in his skin.

I stepped back, looking at my fist. Cheryl laughed.

"Nice punch, baby, right through the Wall Between Worlds." Cheryl hugged me and squeezed my shoulders. "Imagine what you'll be able to do when you actually learn what you're doing with the lands of the dead."

"Where's Kenny?" I asked, looking at the former gang-pile. The three polo-clad guys stood confused, wondering where Kenny was as well...

Then I spotted him, translucent and menacing, stalking toward the chud on the other side of ... the wall between life and death? The Other Side?

I don't know what the fuck it is, all I know is Kenny took out a knife and *killed the fuck out of that guy*. The guy's screams were distant and dim as Kenny went to cutting with this long thin knife, starting at the Achilles tendons and working his way up the body. He sliced and slashed with precision, blood washed out and grey as it sprayed from the apparition who cried and shuddered. Kenny was fast, so fast, ten seconds fast. Back of the knees, the hips, elbows, wrists, neck, the blood pulsing and leaking into the mush which was on the ground on that side of ... the other side, I guess. Wait...

Holy shit, the guy's not dead. Blood's all out of him, pooled all over the floor so far I'm trying not to step in it even on this side, but the guy's not dead. Kenny dropped him in a sloppy pile, propping up the head which keened and hissed. It tried calling out to his friends who couldn't hear him. He cried, gummy tears floating in an unseen wind.

"Pay attention, baby," Cheryl shouted, shoving me out of the way as one of the polo-shirted tools swung on me. He was screaming about where Jimmy went, I guess Jimmy was his friend, but it was hard to hear over the howl from the land of the dead and Jimmy weeping over there. I backed up as the other three came at me. Cheryl did not, shaking her head at them.

"Am I going to have to call your mothers and let them know what naughty boys you are?" she said, shoving one of them backwards. He splashed into the air, ripples in the Wall Between Worlds turning to razors and slicing into his flesh. To his friends, he vanished with a scream. To me, he fell through. Kenny stalked over to him with a knife. The guy didn't bleed here, but the grey, washed-out blood hovered in the barrier before dripping down. He was a slashed and torn mess, ribbons of skin hanging off him or cut clear away, all fallen on the death side of the wall. Kenny went to work, facing the newest arrival towards his friend. This one joined the other one in the hissing, whimpering cry, distant and dim, as they stared at each other with empty eyes.

The others ran.

"Better catch him, baby," Cheryl said as she pointed to one of the fleeing chuds, launching herself after the other one. It was more order than suggestion so I didn't even think about not doing it. He was fast, but I was a middle-distance runner in high school and still kept up running. He shot across the level, weaving through cars, tripping his way around through tight parking jobs and low walls. I kept up a good pace, keeping him in sight, putting on the speed to reach daylight. I caught him on a flight of stairs going up, a leap and trip and stumble which carried us forward…

Through the stairs, through the Wall Between Worlds.

We were in the alcove under the stairs. It wasn't dark. It wasn't light. It was … uniform, bleached away, gray and hazed. My skin, prickly and shimmering from passing through and feeling the ghosts I snorted protecting me from the Wall Between Worlds; his skin, nicked and rent and welling up with the colorless blood from his body. We were in a mush on the floor which kept us 'afloat'. I could feel his legs kicking down and breaking through the surface of the flaky … whatever it was.

He clocked me, hard, in the side of the head. He was strong, lifting strong, working out three days a week strong, and he spun us over so he was on top of me. I managed to wrap my legs around his waist, but he kept on punching me, over and over and over. I grabbed his wrist, slowing the pummeling down. I squeezed, trying to keep his arm in control. He pulled his arm back, away from me, as I pulled his wrist over my head.

He howled in pain as his arm stretched like gum, the forearm long and thin and distended. The cut skin tore more, the greyed-out blood raining down on me. He stopped fighting, his arm a limp whip he tried to nurse in the pain. I scrambled back, him howling more and more as he hugged his arm and screeched at me. I pushed away in a scramble, kicking him in the rib, leaving a dent in his body.

I was ten feet away from him before I realized I was still holding his arm by the wrist and had stretched it out.

I let go, wiping my hand off on my shirt, watching this man with a ten-foot arm and a dent in his ribs stuck halfway in the stairs we had fallen through. I ran, trying to run from the screaming whisper he made, trying to run from the voices telling me I should just stay here since I was already in the lands of the dead, trying to run from the Gen X couple who pulled me into a horror movie. I ran, and I kept on running, up the stairs past the half a ghostly head sticking up out of the steps. I kept on trying to shake off the greyed-out blood which clung to me, scraping away the flakes and dust it rotted into. I kept on running, at first avoiding people outside, the people in the land of the living, but then running through them, being nothing more than a chilled wind in the land of life and light.

And always, the voices in the void whispered at me, telling me to stop and accept where I was. The voices, distant and dim, even if they came from the dying blood on my clothing, from the chunk of flesh I shook out of my hood, from my own blood from the cut above my eye.

"Tommy? Tommy Milgrove, come back, baby," Cheryl's voice carried in the air.

I kept on running, the voice far away.

Fuck, how did they know my real name?

I FELL BACK into the world of the living when the ghosts I snorted wore off. It was a rough fall down a hill in a park, skidding up my pants with mud. The blood and ghost-stuff stuck on me must have stayed on the other side of the Wall Between Worlds, what Cheryl called it. I didn't hear the voices any longer, either the *memento mori* or the murdering soccer mom. I had cash so I caught a bus to get some distance, then I called one of my normie friends to come pick me up and get me back home. They kept on asking if I was OK, and I said I was, but I wasn't, I just watched a husband and wife team drag a bunch of bigots into the lands of the dead and kill them.

I just killed someone in the lands of the dead.

My parents were gone for the weekend, which would give me time to cool down. I showered, trying to talk my way through all this, and repeating myself. I checked under my nails, checked my clothing for flesh and blood, and didn't find anything. I heated up the Chinese food I had from yesterday, greasy, stomach-settling fried rice and BBQ pork.

"Maybe it was the drugs they gave me. They said it was ghosts, maybe it was LSD or something else."

"No, it was ghosts, baby," Cheryl said as she stepped through the Wall Between Worlds into my kitchen.

I crashed back out of the kitchen chair, toward the back door, and ran square into Kenny. He was that one guy in the mosh pit and I bounced off him, ending up on the floor.

"Tommy," Kenny said, reaching down to help me up, "I know this all seems strange—"

"The fuck!" I scrambled off the floor and up the wall, searching for something other than the fork I had as a weapon. "What the fuck are you?"

"We're old-school punks," Kenny said, "who thought we'd be able to retire and let the kids take up the fight against this fascist shit. But *no*, fuckers got lazy and thought because you voted in a Black president meant racism and fascism ended. And here we are."

"We're also necromancers, Tommy," Cheryl added.

"Necro-what?" I asked.

"Necromancers," Kenny said. "We engage in sorcery to communicate and command the dead. Although we've recently been taking a more direct means to deal with fascie trash."

"Killing them?"

"Refining ectoplasm to make a powder which lets us enter the lands of the dead," Kenny said. "And then killing them. In a way, 'snorting ghosts' for anti-fascism."

"It's not like fascists are people," Cheryl said. "And we do differentiate between the LARPers and the more hardcore ones who need to go away. Like those fellows we came across. Two of them beat up a Black woman a few months ago and she later died before she could tell the cops, not like they would do anything."

"How do you know it was them?" I asked.

"We spoke to her," Kenny said.

"But she's dead."

I realized how dumb my question was the moment it came out of my mouth.

"Necromancers," I said. Kenny laughed.

"Yes, necromancers. And to answer your next question," Cheryl said, "we aren't here to kill you or anything. Can you sit down? I think you'd feel better sitting down, you are looking very pale. Did you eat enough? I can cook up something more for you if you want, baby." she already made her way into my fridge, pulling out ingredients.

"Don't worry, she does this with everyone. Uber-mom extreme," Kenny said.

She pulled out chicken and vegetables from the fridge. Kenny put down his backpack. Both she and Kenny went to work, Kenny using the same knife he used on the chuds.

"Don't worry," he said, "everything we harvest stays in the lands of the dead unless we specifically package it."

"Harvest?" I said, slowly sitting back in my chair.

"Need components for necromancy," Kenny said. "Soul parts, body parts. Although having human body parts around is problematic…"

"So," Cheryl picked up where Kenny left off, "we found a way to drag the living into the lands of the dead. We can see the parts, no one else can. And we don't leave a crime scene behind. Just a missing fascist, or racist, or homophobe."

And at that moment, I realized I had two murderers making dinner for me. I was a lot calmer about it than I expected.

"It's like I said," Cheryl said, "it's not like they are people."

Cooking, cooking, plates set, spicy chicken and vegetables with glazed baby potatoes set in front of me.

"Eat up, Tommy," Kenny said. "We have lots to talk about regarding your future."

I ate, slowly, carefully, making sure I looked like I was enjoying it ... it was actually good.

"Don't be surprised, baby," Cheryl said. "It's how I won this guy over," she shoulder-checked Kenny as they both sat down. "That, and we were both looking for the same occult tome and it just seemed like a good idea to share ... everything. Married twenty-eight years. Anyway, we need to talk about your future."

"My future as ... a necromancer?"

"Well, yes," Kenny said, "and as an anti-fascist. You've been active online, and even some local protests, politics and direct action. Mutual aid. You want to help people. You want to do more. We've been tracking you for a while, even had some of our 'friends' keep an eye on you, politely," Kenny added, "to make sure you were committed."

"You had ghosts watching me?" I said.

"Yes," Kenny said. "Intel gathering is important."

"Now," Cheryl said, "we weren't expecting to have a field trip, we thought we'd 'run into' you at the protest and get to know you more. But oops," Cheryl mock-shrugged and put her hands in the air, "bunch of fascists ended up spell components." Kenny picked up his own backpack and opened it, showing bags and bags of chunky, ghostly parts.

"Those boys don't seem very proud now," Kenny said.

"So here we are," Cheryl said. "Baby, you OK?"

I covered my mouth, trying to forget the translucent eyeballs in one of the bags.

"You'll get used to it," Kenny said. "But I saw what you did to the one in the stairs. He was one of the ones who beat up the Black woman. You did a number on him. How did it feel?"

I don't know.

Awful?

Exciting?

Terrifying?

For all the talk about kicking ass people made online, and 'fascists get the wall', actually doing it, tearing skin and yanking arms and denting flesh of someone who deserved it was … empowering?

The right thing to do?

I don't know.

"It needed to be done," I settled with for now, hoping it was the right answer.

Yes, it needed to be done, I assured myself.

"That's the answer we were looking for," Cheryl said. "Don't want someone who can't stomach it, but we don't want someone who is going to get off on it. Next thing you know, you've got a serial killer or a multiple murderer on your hands and that's someone you don't want with necromantic power."

"There is a difference between serial killers and multiple murderers, by the way," Kenny said. "Anyway, eat up, and then we can start your lessons a bit more formally."

"Now?" I said in mid-bite.

"It's a full moon tonight," Cheryl said. "The Wall Between Worlds is thin, it will make it easy to conjure up someone so you can see how it's done."

I laughed, a thought clinging in my head.

"What's so funny?" Cheryl said.

"When I first met you guys, I thought you were trying to drag me into some strange threesome," I said.

"Oh no," Kenny bellowed in laughter, "you're cute, Tommy, but what are you, nineteen? We'd wreck you. You'd be ruined."

Cheryl nodded in agreement. It was like looking at my own mom and dad, if they had killed several fascists today in the lands of the dead.

Well, it's a relief they want me to apprentice under them as a necromancer rather than hook up, I guess…

BEAK

BY SARAH PEPLOE

Florence had been awake since dawn, which always made her feel clean and keen. Ready for anything. The air felt springy, the white boxes painted on the tarmac held the thrill of the starting line, although of course they would not start in the car park but by the war memorial across the road. But now, she could feel the first tugs of exasperation. She didn't want a participation trophy or anything but she did a lot. She had done a lot for today in particular. Florence put together event pages, setting new ones up as soon as old ones were taken down, phoned pubs with function rooms under assumed names, maintained group chats and mailing lists, hired minibuses and designated drivers, organised carshares and childcare. Made picnics.

She did all this happily. Not for her the perennial whine of the resentful woman, Sometimes I don't know why I bother. Florence always knew why she bothered. But if she had ever come close to forgetting it might be now, looking at Kayleigh, having led her behind the empty minibus under the pretence of some nebulously girly chat. What was she thinking?

Kayleigh shrugged. Ever the flipping problem child.

"We're living in this amazing time where we can potentially attract so many new people to the movement," Florence said, "especially women, and you show up looking like something off Jeremy Kyle."

"Yeah I'm not thrilled about it either actually." Kayleigh's voice was muffled and flat. Old blood clogging her nostrils like dead roses. Florence gestured for her to remove the sunglasses. They made it look worse if anything, more obvious. Although it wasn't great without them either. Kayleigh used to be good at makeup, at least the showy over-the-top kind. That photo in the papers which the press had filched from Tumblr, when she got the suspended sentence. Kayleigh, a slutty Dresden doll, straddling a tank at some war museum. Ilsa-ing it up.

But, Florence supposed, concealer and foundation only went so far when the flesh was swollen, when one eye was mostly shut and what you could see of the white was red.

"It's not that bad," Kayleigh said feebly. "Okay, it is bad but no one's going to be looking at me."

"Don't be naïve. Everyone's looking at everyone." Florence gestured with her phone. "For keeps. What happened? Oliver?"

"He was just drunk."

"*Just* drunk?"

"...no. He'd been off it since New Year so that probably explains why he got a bit, you know."

"So Oliver got drunk and high and he beat you?"

"It's not ... it's not that black and white. He'd had a night out, he came home about five–" Kayleigh sighed. She hated how this made her sound like the battleaxe, roused from her ugly sleep, nagging him for having some fun. Which she hadn't been. She thought they'd both been having a laugh about how wired he was. She'd asked after Mike, because it was always Mike for coke, Astrid for weed. Ollie had said Mike wasn't there, it was some mongrel outside Silk's. Then he'd squinted at her face and said What, laughing, and she'd said What back, they were back and forth saying What to each other and they were both laughing, till–

"It was like, a mutually stupid fight," she finished, "it wasn't like he started on me for no reason."

"Doesn't look mutual. I'll get Phil to have a word with him–"

"Don't. Please, Flo, you're gonna make it into a big thing when it isn't. Males fight all the time and the weaker male gets battered, it's a law of nature. It's only feminism that goes on all 'ooh, men and women are equal but if a man hits a woman that's like the most evil thing ever.' So hypocritical. It's just part of life. Would it be understandable if he did it today, no. Was it understandable that he did it when he was off his tits, yes. That's the whole point of loving someone, is you understand each other. He apologised and we had a cuddle and it's fine. I'm fine. Besides–"

"Right," Florence said softly, "I'm glad you two have made up, but you can see that you taking part in the rally today is a not-good situation? Visually?"

"Oh don't fucking–"

"Kayleigh."

"–head-tilt me, you're not the gaffer, you can't tell me whether or not I can be somewhere. If Dave says he doesn't want me here, fair play, I'll sit this one out. If Dave says."

"Do you not think Dave has better things to worry about?"

Something Kayleigh could say neither no nor yes to. She scowled up at Florence, one red eye, one white, like she was trying to turn her into a toad. Kayleigh did still have something of that goth look, though she'd toned it down under Florence's gentle tutelage. But in normal circs when she did a full face it did rather tend towards the stark. And she'd kept her nails, lurid talons in Black Cherry, today. And her bracelets, almost up to the elbows over the skinny black polo neck she was wearing, silver bracelets bedecked and engraved with runes, crosses, skulls. They clinked now as she wrapped her hands round her upper arms, cradling herself. Florence could tell she was starting to see sense. It was important to let her get there on her own.

"I was looking forward to it," she said dejectedly.

Florence gave her a hug, careful of her face. "They also serve who only stand and wait, hun."

They went back to the rest of the group, who had spread out around the car park as more people had arrived. Florence shook hands, gave chaste hugs, asked after wives and kids. As she weaved through the gathering she felt Kayleigh's presence at her side like a tumour, silent and wobbly.

Dave, in the blue herringbone three-piece he'd bought out of the last crowdfund, was at the heart of it all, talking to Chocks, or rather to his camera. Chocks panned away, saying "Here we all are, raring to go, no, ah, no counter-protesters yet, eh Dave?" and the two men shared a chuckle. Florence waved and smiled at the lens and positioned herself in front of Kayleigh–but she wasn't there. Florence had heard her clink. Hadn't she? Florence turned back and forth. She couldn't see Oliver either, but over to her left there was a knot of men and flags and a laugh like a sea lion in heat emanating from it, which was probably him.

She looked back over at Chocks, admiring the ease with which he moved the camera to look outwards or at himself, to skip gracefully over certain people, an extension of his will. She thought she had glimpsed Kayleigh's hair against the stark white and red of those flags, but she was back now, hovering again at Florence's shoulder.

Florence grabbed her arm and said "I just had a ff–antastic idea."

SHE WENT and okayed it with Phil first, who took it to Dave. "Yeah, good stuff," Dave said. "When life gives you lemons, eh." He was clapping Phil on the back but he was looking approvingly at Florence. "That's my girl," Phil said. Winked at her like they were teenagers again.

The group were mobilising, now, the banner unfurled by Joanne and Sally, the flags shouldered by everyone. Almost everyone. Marshall, Tug, David (not Dave), Darren et cetera, stood as always at the edges, hands free, feet shoulder-width apart, marvellously still and ready. And Marshall's dogs good as gold, waiting. They made her feel safe. Not that she'd have to worry, today. She got the minibus keys from Darren, then said goodbye to Joanne and Sally, and the silent, clingy new girlfriends that one or two of the younger lads had brought along. She'd have to make more of an effort with them in the future.

They all took up a spirited chant and crossed the road to the memorial. Kayleigh and Florence returned to the minibus.

"Ok," Florence said to Kayleigh. "I'll keep you company while the rally's on. We'll stay in the bus, I'll, ah, freshen"–she gestured at Kayleigh's face–"all this up a bit, and we'll say you were jumped by the other lot. Put it on the socials."

For a moment Florence thought Kayleigh might say no. She'd be humiliated, having the swollen mess of herself splashed across Facebook. But that was exactly why she was going to say yes, Florence could tell. There was an obscure but unmistakable pride dawning in her white eye. Ollie had taken her face from her. Doing this would give it back.

"Break the internet, sort of thing."

"Precisely." She unlocked the door with a beep. "So you won't be there. You'll be everywhere else. A call to arms."

Kayleigh got in the passenger seat, Florence the driver's seat. She handed Kayleigh a pack of micellar wipes from her handbag. Florence always had everything.

It was odd, watching Kayleigh take her makeup off. The everyday memory of doing the same thing thrummed in Florence's own still fingers. Florence of course favoured the lightest of cosmetic touches, make-up that didn't look made up–and a bit more besides, but likewise nothing Florence had done *looked* done. Most of it was hydration and skin care anyway. Just a dab of reassuringly expensive Botox and a good nose, straight as a die, neat as a pin.

Kayleigh turned her head this way and that in the vanity mirror, folding and refolding the peach-stained wipe between her nails. She sniffed. "Who are you gonna say it was?"

Florence tsk-ed at her obliviousness. "Antifa."

"Nah. You need to go specific. A paki or a pronoun cunt."

"Kayleigh."

"Sorry. Pronoun vagina. Beard and a dress anyway."

Incorrigible. Florence giggled despite herself. It was nice. Here in the minibus with Kayleigh, up to tricks. It was just nice. Kayleigh dropped the soiled wipe out of the window and turned to Florence. Offering her clean face with its inky clouds and a big plump jowl on one side.

Florence reached forward and took the other woman's nose between finger and thumb, just under the bridge. She rolled and pressed like it was a piece of clay. Kayleigh's nails dug into the grey seat. This was pain she could get a handle on at least. The shape of it. Knowing it would definitely end as soon as she bled. Not like when she was on her living room floor with her nose feeling bigger than her face. Ollie's rings vampire-biting. The noise she couldn't make a filthy salt soup at the back of her throat.

She didn't bleed. So Florence reached into Kayleigh's nostril with a little finger, probing up there with her sensible nude manicure, till she found some resistance, a crusty, grainy slope which she worked at gently like an archaeologist, leaning in close, close–

"Were dere dogs in here?" Kayleigh asked.

"Yeah, Marshall brought Blut and Boden with him. Do you need some antihistam–"

Kayleigh sneezed.

A quivery silence. Kayleigh's nostrils were streaming blood now. Fat red droplets sat on her lips, cheeks, and chin. She also wore an expression of mortified horror.

"...well," Florence said, "that'll do it."

Kayleigh burst out in shrill terrified laughter. "Oh god I'm sorry! Oh no–I got it on you–ew."

Florence laughed too, more comfortably. She could feel the warm wet freckling her own face but she couldn't be cross; Kayleigh looked wonderful. Like she'd literally just been saved from the clutches of some unwashed degenerate.

"Can't argue with results. Ok. Cry."

"Huh?"

Florence held her phone up. "Just start crying and I'll take a few."

"How?"

Florence realised she could not tell her. How do you cry? It was like telling her how to put lipstick on.

Kayleigh tried to think of enough pain, but found she could only remember that she had been in enough pain. The pain itself was harder to call back. She tried for emotional pain but that didn't work either. It was way down low beneath inches of cicatrisation, hot and wet and unsurvivable as the core of the earth. She couldn't reach.

She remembered release. Dragging in a big breath. Metallic and snotty. He'd climbed off her and got to his feet so sudden she thought, briefly, someone might have turned up. Popped over for a dawn cuppa. His Mum did have a key. Kayleigh was crying, then, pathetic but she couldn't help it. It felt like he'd split her skull.

Ollie had left the room, his feet soft on the carpet. Then nothing. She might have blacked out but just for a second. There was the toilet flushing and the sink running. Then he was back. He had a cold wet towel. Shh, you're ok. Kneeling over her, thumbing her mouth open. His fingers inside her. Checking her like a horse. Nothing broken. No harm done.

The towel clammy and slack on her shoulder, suddenly. Thuds. She cringed. But it was Ollie punching himself. Shit, shit, he was saying, piece of fucking shit. She took his wrists in her hands gently, careful of her nails. He collapsed into her breasts. She held him while he wept.

In the minibus now she gurned and heaved as best she could, and took the clicks as proof of Florence's satisfaction.

FLORENCE BROUGHT a blisterpack of Loratadine and a minipack of tissues out of her handbag, took one of the latter for herself, and then handed both to Kayleigh. Florence didn't have allergies, which she took as proof of her own mother's good sense and lack of snowflakey neuroses, letting her play in the mud and whatnot. Odd then that her nose felt tickly when she wiped it, cleaning off the blood Kayleigh had covered her in.

She lifted her phone from her thigh. Kayleigh looked back at her from the screen, all contortion and damage. Beautiful. Of course, some smart alec somewhere might check the time it was first posted and then sift through some of the other members' social media like Zapruder footage for a chance glimpse of Kayleigh already bruised. He might read her injuries and say that under their dazzle of blood they didn't look brand new. Let him. Let them all sputter and wring their hands, let them prove beyond a shadow of a doubt it didn't happen. It did not matter. The lie had gotten there first and would always be there first, gold medal in its fist.

She opened the relevant Facebook page and selected the best photo, where Kayleigh had looked up, her open eye limpid and imploring as a saint's. She started typing, Religion of peace, crying emoji, angry emoji–

A bead of blood landed on the screen. She swiped it away. More replaced it. A quick little patter in a triangle formation. Must've missed some–

She looked at herself, strangely reflected. The planes of her jaw and cheeks half-visible in Kayleigh's temples, in the squinch and shine of her eyes. And just above, in the black dark-mode screen that Florence preferred, she could see a shiny bead of blood crawling from her own right nostril.

As she took another tissue to wipe it away she felt it creep, distinctly, over her top lip. There was no pain but it was definitely coming out of her; it wasn't Kayleigh's. She was about to turn to her and say something like I've heard of women coming on at the same time but this is ridiculous, when Kayleigh's hip pocket buzzed against the seat. Kayleigh wiped her nose hurriedly, licked her lips and tossed her hair.

"It'll be Ollie, he'll just want to know where I am."

"He knows where you are."

"Yeah but he'll want proof." Florence realised Kayleigh had made herself camera-ready. She smiled with her crust-lined, spit-glossed mouth. "It's just a thing we do."

"Oh for goodness sake, if you shouted he could hear you." Although that might not be true. It was getting loud over there, an indistinct roar without the beat of their normal chants. Kayleigh was frowning lightly at her.

"...no," she said. "He didn't come. I was gonna tell you before. He's still, you know. A bit. I didn't even see him this morning. He was still in bed. I got a lift with Sally–" her voice faltered, looking at Florence. Her working eye went wide.

Florence touched her upper lip, either side of her philtrum. Both fingertips came back scarlet.

Kayleigh looked stricken, torn between Florence and her phone. And she was bleeding again. She croaked, "I have to, I have to g-get it–" and fumbled her phone out of her pocket. Florence was dealing with her own nose, bowing her head, pinching just below the bridge. So she didn't see Kayleigh frown at the name on the screen, choose answer rather than video call, but she heard what came out of the phone, a woman's voice, no, a woman's noise, syllables broken up by whooping sobs. "Irene?" Kayleigh said haltingly.

There was a dreadful weight settling between Florence's eyes, a pressure that her clamping fingers did not shift, that the flow of blood did not relieve. Her free fingers were suddenly greased with blood that, however hard she squeezed, would not stop flowing. She felt the first uncoiling of terror. She'd heard, with rhinoplasty, sometimes the surgeons made a mistake. They left a big old clot of scar tissue up there which would lean into some artery quietly for years until one day whoosh. Like the boulder in Indiana Jones. Taking you with it. It had to be that, right, some medical malpractice, someone she would sue, it had to, you couldn't catch a nosebleed–

There was a crack from her left as, slick as soap, Kayleigh's phone slid into the footwell. Fat droplets, cherry-dark, cherry-sized, pattered down onto her palm, slicking the heel of her hand and then disappearing into the black of her polo neck and jeans, unceasingly. Kayleigh's face was pointed forward, but she didn't seem to be looking at anything. "What have you done to me?" she whimpered.

"Me?" Florence hissed. Hadn't Kayleigh just sprayed her filthy dirty blood into the most vulnerable, most inside-out parts of Florence, her mouth, her tear ducts? The revulsion of it was unbelievable, like that time some poof had opened his AIDSy veins into the ketchup dispenser at McDonalds or Burger King or whichever worked better for the story, which is why they only have sachets now. But Kayleigh was repeating her question, her head balloon-bobbing and not looking at Florence, and she was saying Baby. "Baby, what have you done?"

"Just–calm down." Florence pressed down on Kayleigh's back, trying to make her lean forward. "Who's Irene?"

"Ollie's Mum." Kayleigh's white eye rabbit-rolling, full of horrors. "You see. It wasn't Mike."

And then as Florence frowned at her, Kayleigh's eye changed from white to red, as swiftly and neatly as if a bubble had been blown from within, or a slide had been changed. She reached up to her face, her breathing quick and violent.

"It's–it's ok, it's nothing to worry about, it happens, it's normal." Florence leaned closer, getting bled on again. They were both caked now, although more obviously in Florence's case with her champagne blouse, her mushroom slacks. "Eyes, nose, it's all connected, isn't it–"

Kayleigh's laugh, again. High and joyless as a scream. It went on and on. The blood spurted from her in time with the noise. Keeping her eyes on Kayleigh, Florence groped for her phone, where it had landed against the gearstick. As she jabbed 9s, she looked up where Kayleigh was looking, out of the windscreen. Her eyes caught a dash of blue against the Portland stone of the memorial. Dave, backing away up the steps. She could see his deep pink face, and his mouth a little dark goldfish gape. At the foot of the steps, they all seemed to be fighting, turning on each other. Then she realised they were clinging to each other. Flags pooled on the ground. Marshall fought his way free, stumbled, turned towards Dave. Sneezed a parabola of blood into him.

Dave sat suddenly like a baby still getting the hang of walking. He lifted his hands to his face and brought them away with stringy, red ropes from his mouth, nostrils, eyes.

Her phone was gone from her hand. Like Kayleigh's, somewhere down by her feet, behind the brake, or the accelerator? She folded herself down there to grope for it, which brought a wave of nauseating pain. Her vision swam. She came back up empty handed, retching strands of dark, ferrous spittle.

"See what I think is Ollie didn't know him but he knew Ollie."

"What?"

"Outside Silk's."

"What?"

"Connected, you said. You said–" Kayleigh's voice burbled and hissed, a straw in a milkshake, "it's all connected. All hidden. I just, you know. I was looking forward to it. I wanted to have a good one. So."

Again, that terrified, abject, begging laugh. She held her hands up before her like a shrug or an offering. Her nails looked like her teeth. Her silver bracelets clinked. Florence noticed one of them in particular, one of those big ones with the excessively chunky clasp that could open secretly at the side like a book. Her palms were filling with clots, then a tooth, then another. "And then when you told me I wasn't going I thought. Share the wealth. You know."

It occurred to Florence that this was all her fault. Whenever anything didn't go to plan it was always, when you got down to it, something Florence should have thought of, some angle she should have considered, something she hadn't asked. It was very easy for Florence to understand this, so it was particularly aggravating to her that she'd only just realised it, regarding this situation. She knew about Kayleigh's allergies, and her weaknesses, and she had assumed and she had not asked, and it had been Florence's fucking fantastic idea. All her fault.

But I can, yet, Florence thought, I can. There was nothing after those words, but she was sure she could do whatever it was. She always adapted and multitasked and fixed, she made do and made the best of. She was just so good at that sort of thing. She grabbed stickily at the door lock but her hands, white and red and flappy as flags, didn't seem to work right. There were little voices. Irene, still, or the 999 dispatcher. Her phone, Kayleigh's phone, distant as moons. She thought, Phil, and she thought I did hit Post, right? I must've.

Then the minibus door opened and she fell with it, and then there was only the pain, through the middle of her head like a lead-lined well, an endless, open, clanging plummet. Nothing else possible.

Florence was cold, suddenly. A burnished black-red puddle on the tarmac in front of her. She dropped to her knees–one knee; her other leg was wrapped in the seat belt–then her elbows in it. It grew with her every move, until she could not move. She sunk onto her face. She heard Kayleigh's milkshake noises behind her, heard them gutter and stop. She saw her blood, vibrant on the painted line beneath her eyes. And last of all a flood of bubbles tiny and orange as caviar, popping into nothingness. Her lips half-forming soundless, orphaned words. They only have sachets now.

BLOOD & HONOR
BY SAM RICHARD

As Randy walked up to Phil's derelict house, she was unsure what to anticipate. They hadn't spoken in over two decades, and she didn't know what had drawn her to him. She even ignored his initial message. Her past was best left as bad memories she suppressed, but his second message gave her chills, so she called the number he'd sent. There was something about the panic in his voice, the way he spoke with such exhausted intensity. When she was honest with herself, she recognized that the slur in his speech really worried her.

Like he might not live to tomorrow.

Reluctantly, she got in her car and drove as quickly as she could. Fortunately, it was only a few hours from Minneapolis to just outside of Lamberton. Not a place she anticipated spending her Sunday, but perhaps family *was* family. And Phil had been the only one who was truly decent to her growing up.

A series of putrid smells hit her as she pushed open the already cracked door. Coughing and gagging, she did her best to call out to Phil as she stepped inside. Dense clusters of flies covered the various surfaces of the kitchen; dark brown splotches and streaks covered the floor, countertops, and cabinets. More the scene of a grisly murder than a livable home.

Something tugged in the back of her brain. It told her to run. To get in her car, lock the doors, and call the police. Before she could, a voice called her name from deeper within the house.

"Randy, is that you?" It was hoarse and quiet, barely louder than a whisper. She imagined it belonging to someone approaching their hundredth birthday. "Fuck, I'm so glad you came. Can you come in here?"

After a beat of hesitation, Randy decided that she had come this far, might as well see if there was something she could do to help. Given their vast years apart, she didn't know if Phil had a partner or children, or if he was disabled or living with a chronic illness or trying to overcome a disease. She wondered if whoever had been helping him had left or passed on themselves. And given the state of the place, she figured whatever it was had been going on for quite a while.

Holding her breath, she stepped into the darkened room off the kitchen. Even with her nose closed off, she could taste it. Not merely the scent of illness, but of infection. Rot. Decay. The sickly-sweet smell of sunbaked roadkill or dead squirrels trapped inside the walls. But larger. Human.

Dim sunlight peeked through the heavy curtains, sending a few lines of light cascading across the filthy wooden floors. She was standing in the dining room, beyond that the living room. A figure sat on a large couch, staring at her in the relative darkness. Doing her best to avoid stepping in any of the debris that littered the floor, she slowly walked toward the figure.

"Phil, is that you? Are you okay?"

"Yes, yes. Please, come have a seat. Thank you for coming on such short notice," he paused. "...honestly, I can't believe that you actually came."

Randy spotted a clean, empty chair across from the couch, directly facing her cousin. Like it was set up for an interrogation. Between it and the couch sat a small, cluttered table, though Randy couldn't make out what was on it in the dark. A handful of boxes were on either side of it.

Angry flies swarmed everywhere.

She sat and studied Phil. He was covered in a pile of blankets, more mass of cloth than man. His features were difficult to discern in the dim lighting. The brutal stench wrapped itself around her, and Randy forced herself to not gag. The world could be so cruel to people with medical conditions, and she didn't want to offend him; she didn't want to make him feel less than human. From the state of things, it certainly didn't look like he wanted to be living like this.

"I don't know what to say, and I don't mean to offend you at all— so please don't take it that way—but do you need me to call a doctor, or a nurse? Is that why you tracked me down?"

Without a beat he started speaking. "So, my dad died a few years ago, lousy fucking bastard. Managed to hang on for a good decade longer than we all thought he would. Coronary Artery Disease. Had that shit for ages. Wouldn't stop smoking, never took care of himself, drank all the time. I always thought he'd pop young, but the old fucker just kept going, kept pulling us down around him, too. Do you remember what he would say to us when we were kids?"

Randy let her guard down. It was wholly unpleasant to revisit that era of her life, but she also rarely had the opportunity, especially with someone else who lived through it. She cleared her throat, "Uhh, yeah. He always told us that we were the future. That they were fighting to give us the keys to the kingdom of heaven or some shit. It always felt Arthurian, but I can't recall how he phrased it."

"Exactly! The importance he placed on us; truly bizarre considering how he treated us, really. You know, I didn't know that other people's parents didn't do that until I was in my early twenties. Figured that was what parents did. Figured everyone said grace before eating dinner, pledged their allegiance to The Christian Flag as well as the stars and stripes, and talked about securing a future for their children. Thought that was the most normal thing in the world.

"Not you, though. Right? Figured you wised up early, figured that was why you left. You know, they told us you were a—and pardon my use of this word, I'm merely quoting your dad—'a dyke' and that you ran off to join a commune or something like that."

The fetid air constricted around Randy's throat. She had anticipated this possibility but hoped it wasn't the case. She kicked herself for hoping things were different as deep, unhealed wounds tore their way to the surface. He was still just like them and had brought her here to torture her for who she was. Her eyes dimmed with sorrow and anger.

Phil shifted painfully as he spoke through a grunt, "Whoa, whoa there. I'm sorry. I really did not mean to offend you. I realize that we haven't seen each other in a while, but please know that I did not bring you here to harass you about who you are. Fuck, I don't even know who you are. I sincerely don't know if that was true or he was just talking out of his ass, but please know that if it bears any truth I am not judging that. I know what they were like. I know what I was like when we were kids. I have done everything in my power to not be like them anymore, to not be who I was. That's actually why I wanted to talk with you."

Randy collected herself, the waves of panic and iced out veins subsided as a series of unhealthy, wet coughs erupted from Phil's mouth. Flies buzzed as he coughed.

"Look, I appreciate that you didn't bring me here to judge me, but are you sure you don't want me to call a doctor or nurse, or maybe another close friend of yours? I'm not, by the way. A 'dyke.' I'm bi, so I guess it's a half-truth, or something. My dad found a note I wrote to a girl I had a crush on. Totally innocent stuff, too. He freaked out. Called me an 'abomination,' and I bailed as soon as I could after that. Wasn't a commune either, just like him to say that. The place was a halfway house for homeless youth. Not exactly an unholy communist utopia."

As the words spilled out of her, the tension dropped off her shoulders. She recognized this was still a wholly bizarre interaction, but she trusted that he wasn't trying to hurt her. It had been a long time since she'd been able to say that about a member of her family.

"Makes sense…" Phil slurred his words. "No, really I'm fine

enough. I just need you to sit here and talk with me. I promise that I'll let you know what's going on and why I asked you to come here.

"So anyhow, seeing as our childhoods were nothing less than completely fucked up, you were the only one who I thought would understand. Who might be willing to help.

"We both know that our fathers were bad people. And shit, I guess I hadn't thought about this before, but you do know your father is dead, right?"

Randy stayed silent, processing the information. She did know. More in a vague, impersonal way. An old friend who she occasionally spoke to sent her the newspaper article four years ago. Car accident, dead on impact. Likely drunk with a backseat full of guns. A pipe bomb had gone off, so there wasn't much left of him to find, but the pulverized bottles on the driver side seat didn't leave much to the imagination.

She hadn't cried when she found out. It was all so distant, and her rage and pain and self-preservation were too strong to allow her to give any tears for a man who lived such an abhorrent, hate-filled life. She filed it away into a logical section of her mind she titled 'Things I am Aware Of' and tried not to think of it. And when she was alone, in the dark of night and unable to sleep, sometimes it would creep up on her. But not for long before she reminded herself that maybe she hadn't really had a father; or maybe her father had truly died years before she was born.

Still, Phil saying it made his death even more real. Hearing it from the mouth of someone who also knew him. Someone who knew what he was like and what he did. A single tear rolled down Randy's cheek as she tried to connect with Phil's eyes in the darkness. But she found nothing but a subtle glow of skin lighter than the blankets that wrapped his body.

"...I did, but only because of the news. I've never heard anyone talk about it, at least not someone who wasn't on TV reporting on it. Sorry. What a fucking bastard. Fuck." Randy wiped her cheek.

"I'm sorry, I shouldn't have dropped it on you like that, but I really wasn't sure if you talked to anyone. I kind of assumed you were completely detached."

"I mean, I am. Just that one friend. The year I left, I tried to stay in touch with my mom. Honestly, I felt terrible, like I had abandoned her and left her to fend for herself with that monster, but the more we talked, the more the conversations became inquisitions, like he was standing next to her with a list of questions, trying to track down where I was and bring me back. At one point, I believe due to him, she threatened to call the police and have me listed as a runaway or missing child, but it was like a month before I turned eighteen, so I just stopped talking with them and figured that if they actually did that, by the time it became a problem I would be a legal adult and no one could do shit.

"Jesus, I feel like I've never said most of this out loud before. When it's your own life, it's hard to see how truly fucked it is, isn't it?"

"It took me years to unpack. And if I'm being honest with myself, I didn't do the best job at it. I wouldn't be here if it weren't for my friend Lance. I'd probably be dead with the rest of 'em." Phil lazily swatted a few flies off his face, sending a fresh wave of rot to Randy. "Wait, you know your mom got remarried then? After your dad passed, right?"

"...no. What? Is he ... is he a nice person? A *good* person?"

"I have no idea. Got an email from my brother a couple of years ago. He was mad about how she 'didn't even wait until Uncle Brad was cold before jumping on a new dick.' Some bullshit like that. He emailed me for a while. Not sure how he tracked me down, but I never replied."

"Shit," Randy laughed through more tears. "Well, this really is a fucked up family reunion, isn't it? Discussing all the normal things regular folks might at a picnic hosted by the grand matriarch of the family, everyone making sure to let everyone else know who's dead and which of their parents remarried..."

Phil let out a loud, boisterous laugh until another coughing fit left him winded. He reached over for a glass bottle next to him on the pile of blankets and awkwardly opened it with one hand, taking a long pull while staring in Randy's direction. His arm appeared unnaturally gaunt in the dim light. A small swarm of flies flew off it as he moved.

"I'd offer you some, but this is all I have and I'm gonna need to make it last.

"So anyhow, not long after you left—good for you by the way, I should have done that—what, a few years later, was Hurricane Katrina? I guess it's not important to map out the entire timeline—"

"Oh yeah, that sounds right, I left in 2002, Katrina was something like 2004 or 2005? Shit, sorry to interrupt."

"It's fine, sorry I haven't had a visitor in a while, and I know I'm rambling. Don't mind me, the meds and the alcohol make my thoughts swim."

"Are you supposed to be drinking on meds? Can't that be, like, really fucking bad?"

"Typically, yes, I think—at least depending on the med. But don't worry about it, it's okay with these. Just makes me a little fuzzy, so I'm sorry if I meander in my story or if I repeat myself." Randy sensed a crooked grin awkwardly crawl across his face.

"Anyhow, during Katrina. Do you remember Patrick, my dad's best friend? ...doesn't matter. So, after Katrina started, Patrick, who is a good old southern boy, just like our dads, decided to crash into New Orleans with a group of friends to see what kind of trouble they could get into during the chaos.

"I figured this meant stealing some TVs or maybe some cases of whiskey from abandoned liquor stores, maybe grabbing some money somewhere in the chaos. But no, he cooked up this idea, and I don't think it was his alone. Probably cribbed from some StormFront message board post; at the very least, I know that they weren't the only jackoffs with this idea.

"My dad wakes me up one morning and is like, 'hey asshole, get up, we gotta go, grab some shit and meet me in the truck in five.' I don't know what's what, probably hung over and out of it, but you know my dad, not good to keep him waiting. Especially not his 'no good son, still living at home at twenty-two.' So, I grab a bag and throw some questionably clean clothes in it and jump in the truck.

"Waiting for me are both our dads, Patrick, and his kid, Kenny. We start driving. Now I have no idea when I get in the truck that this isn't like, 'let's go up north with some beers at a cabin,' or some shit. This is driving—virtually nonstop—from southern Illinois to New Orleans.

"We were in the car for what felt like a whole day—though it must have been like ten hours, max. The whole time we're driving, they're all riled up, raring to go. You know how they were. Cheap beers and a bottle of some bottom shelf whiskey being passed between us, rowdy banter, talking about killing some of 'those people' and using all sorts of words that I'm ashamed to say I spent the better part of my life using. Words I cannot bring myself to say anymore.

"I figure it's just talk, and drunk talk at that, but the closer we get to the city—and the more the oncoming traffic on the other side of the divider became congested and chaotic—the more the jokes become serious; the more I begin to realize that this was very real. That we were headed to New Orleans to basically, in my dad's words, 'kick off the motherfucking race war.'

"And that's what we tried to do."

Randy sat in silence. The day's heat had made the foul smell more intense and recognizing what Phil had said, what he meant, made her nauseous. Bile rose in her throat, and she pushed it back down, refusing to throw up in front of him.

"I know that's a lot, but I need you to know. I need you to know what I've done. Look. I don't have much time left, and I can't die without doing something about it. I need you to know, and I need you to tell them." Phil's silhouette slouched as he spoke.

"I ... I don't know if I can do this." Randy's legs screamed at her to get up, to run back to her car and drive away and never think about any of this ever again. She began to stand.

"I'm sorry. I know this is so much to put on you, but I don't have anyone else. Please. Please, Randy, help me make this right and you'll never have to think about me or our family ever again. I just need you to know ... I need you to know what we did."

Breathing heavily through her nostrils, Randy sat back down and tried to collect her thoughts. Tried to open the most compassionate parts of her towards the only family member she'd spoken to in nearly twenty goddamn years.

"Ok. I help you and I walk out that door and you don't call me or text me or message me again."

Nodding, Phil continued as disturbed flies buzzed frantically around him before settling again, "Agreed. So, we rolled into the city, and it was all but deserted. Areas of it were completely closed off or flooded and the winds were whipping through like nothing I'd ever seen before. Rocked the goddamn truck with such a fury that I was sure we were going to tip or be thrown clean across the road.

"Patrick had some friends we were supposed to meet, but I guess no one anticipated the cell towers being affected by the storm, so we were never able to talk with them. I later saw a video of one of them, drunk off his ass at a party, loudly boasting about all the black folks he'd killed that week during the storm. Folks around him laughing and cheering like he's talking about getting laid. Like I said, I know there were others.

"For days we drove around, drinking warm beer and living off beef jerky and MREs. Your dad called it, 'hunting.' First person we came across was a young black guy walking along the side of the road. He was soaking wet and limping, like he'd fallen into the flood and gotten tossed around or something. He was babbling and looked like he was in a lot of pain. My dad and Patrick jumped out of the truck and shot him right in the face without saying a fucking word." Phil's slurred voice trembled.

"They snagged his wallet—which my dad labeled a trophy—and pushed his body under some debris. As far as I know, no one found him. I figure he washed out to sea.

"I damn near threw up. They got back in the truck and I was freaking out. Screaming, crying, god knows what. I don't remember. My dad smacked me, screaming at me to stop being a bitch, told me he brought me to make a man out of me. Told me I needed to do this for the Aryan race.

"I know you know this. I was deep into that stuff, along with the rest of 'em. Didn't see certain folks as human; couldn't see their humanity because my own was covered in so much hate. I'm not gonna pretend I went into this all blameless and pure. I'd beaten plenty of guys with baseball bats and brass knuckles. Stabbed a few, even. Spent some time in prison, had the tattoos. I lived the life. But not that. I'd never seen someone go from being alive to simply not over a single goddamn second."

"Jesus Christ," shot out of Randy's mouth followed by silence.

"Look, I'm not blameless. I didn't stop them. I didn't fight them. I knew what they were capable of, so when the next one came, I buried everything that made me human—what little there was—and I joined them. Figured it was them or me. Too stupid to realize it would still be them and me, eventually.

"The next one was a woman. Hispanic, I think. It was hard to tell in the rain and I tried to avoid her eyes because I knew I couldn't do it if we made contact. We watched her dip into a building, trying to find shelter from the storm. We all got out and followed, Patrick leading the charge.

"She was in an abandoned diner. They had barely done anything to close the place down; may as well have left the door wide open. She heard us come in and asked for help. Our fathers grabbed me, put a gun in my hand, and pushed me towards her. Told me it was her or me. I know I shouldn't have. I know I should have fought or ran, but everything I believed crept up on me. She was less than human. She was trying to ruin our country, trying to take our jobs. She was trying to destroy our race and way of life. She was ruining America and the purity of the gene pool. I repeated the fourteen words over and over in my head, like a fucking mantra.

"I kept my eyes on her neck as she cried. Lifting the gun, I didn't even hesitate to pull the trigger, hoping—praying—that we were right and that this was a just, righteous cause. A part of my soul died that day. And I know I can never get it back. I know I can never undo what I did. Those people are dead. We did that.

"I did that.

"And there's no coming back from it. There were four more. I don't think you need the details because they're not important. What's important is that I did that to them. What was important were their lives. They are dead because of me, and their families don't know what happened. All they know is that their brothers and sisters and daughters and sons and mothers and fathers and husbands and wives and friends and cousins and on and on and on, aren't ever coming back. They don't even have bodies to bury.

"I know because I've looked. I have the trophies. Found 'em in the garage, tucked away behind old paint cans after my dad died. Always wondered if he'd ever use them to blackmail Patrick or your dad or myself, but he never did. Never talked about it either. Not even when drunk. It was like it had never happened. Like we never spent a week killing six people during a devastating hurricane. But I found their missing posters, their pleading families, their broken parents and siblings and spouses."

Phil slowly shifted in the darkness and a lamp snapped on, filling the room with harsh white light. It took a second for her eyes to adjust. Randy expected her cousin to look as he always had, just add twenty-years and a rough life, but the person staring back at her barely looked alive; barely looked human.

What had once been an enviable mop of blond atop his head was replaced by a few wispy patches of scraggly white hair. But it was his face, his eyes, that revealed the most. Deep sunken dark rings surrounded beet red eyes. His skull was almost completely defined under his paper-thin, pallid skin. Drool dripped from his swollen, chapped mouth as he stared at Randy.

Buzzing flies littered his face and head.

He took another awkward slug from the bottle and then reached to the other side of himself and opened a bottle of pills. It took a minute because he only had one hand. One arm. Randy looked down as Phil clumsily swallowed a handful of pills and drowned them in the last of the liquor. He didn't have any legs.

In one swift motion, Phil removed the blankets, fully revealing himself to her. Hordes of flies fluttered around the room. The overpowering scent of old rot hit her first, followed by the horrifying reality in front of her.

"This is what I've been able to do myself. I guess I didn't think about it too much when I started, but it was inevitable that there would be things I couldn't do alone." He let out a chuckle.

An angry nub protruded out of his shoulder, the skin was charred and inflamed; green pus dripped onto the abrasive '70s sofa fabric below. His legs were much the same. Swollen stumps, one badly burnt, the other with dark red veins growing up the wound towards his hip. Maggots squirmed on the sofa below him, some dangling from the infected wounds.

"I did that one first," he gestured to the veins. "Didn't know about cauterization yet. I'm no doctor, believe it or not." He laughed abruptly, tears streaming down his cheeks. "This whole thing was trial and error. Figured it was gonna kill me anyhow, so might as well jump in with both feet ... err, well I guess not anymore, huh?" He let out a manic cackle which turned into pained wheezing.

The shock wore Randy like a suit. Nothing made sense, wasn't real. This was a nightmare. Reality had fractured.

"See these boxes? First three are done. Addressed 'em myself and everything. But these last three coolers, I'm gonna need your help on those. Ya see, I can't do my other arm myself, for obvious reasons. Nor can I do my skin, figure I'd pass out too quickly from shock or blood loss and this whole thing would be for naught. And my head, too, obviously. That's the last one, ya know.

"I need this. I know I'm asking more than ever should be asked of anyone ever, but I need these people to see my penance. My absolution. My repentance and contrition. What I took from them is irreplaceable, I know that. But if I can give them myself, well, I figure that means more than rotting in a prison cell until I die. This will show them how sorry I am. How I've changed.

"Remember where we came from, who they tried to make us be. I know you got out. But I didn't. Not until my dad died. Lance helped me. He showed me that good people exist. He showed me that I could be good, too. Look. I've done terrible things. Not just that weekend, though that certainly was the worst. Things I can never undo. Please. Please, Randy, please help me show these families that I repent.

"The pills are kicking in so it's now or never. Thank you for…" Phil trailed off, a stream of drool dribbling out of his mouth before his body went limp, slouching in place.

On the table between them was a circular saw, gloves, plastic wrap, and a knife. Three coolers sat on the floor next to the table, each in its own pre-labeled box. An envelope sat atop each cooler.

She knew it was crazy. She knew it was wrong or immoral or monstrous or beyond the absolute-fucking-pale. But she also felt it deep within. The way Phil talked, his final wish. His last rites. She thought about their fathers, the world they grew up in. A childhood only meant to spread more damage and pain and hate. And she wondered if there was any better choice of contrition. Frankly, she couldn't think of one.

So, with tears in her eyes, she picked up the saw and turned it on.

The arm was shockingly easy, just the whirring of the blade against the bones made her queasy. The head was worse. It was all so much more personal, but it went fast, spitting blood all over the room, leaving a perfect red horizon line on the wall behind where Phil sat.

His flesh was a whole other story. Once she started cutting, the shock wore off. She saw her blood-coated hands, the decaying gore in front of her, and she puked.

This wasn't right. Randy tried to breathe, to stop herself, but she saw his eyes in her mind, she heard his voice, his story. This was a man beyond despair. A man in need of some redemption.

She resumed cutting.

Randy wasn't a doctor, so Phil's flesh came off in uneven chunks. Her imperfect slices weren't clean enough, leaving skin stretched and torn and tattered. She also didn't expect there to be so much pus, so many pockets of rot and decay. So many maggots.

She had been talking to a man long dead.

After packing everything up, Randy realized that she had tossed the letters aside in no discernible order. Opening them all to verify the addresses, she couldn't help but scan what he'd written.

Like everything that day, it felt horribly wrong and invasive, so she forced herself to put them away and get everything packed up. But despite her reservations, she couldn't help but catch the final line on each note.

Sorry about all the blood.

BOX OF TEETH
BY JOHN BALTISBERGER

Eduardo checked Ms. Detmold's catheter. A lot of the other attendants hated catheter duty, but it wasn't so bad. Ms. Detmold's was clean. Usually by evening it was all crusty with dried discharge. It probably meant that it had not been clean earlier today, that she had pulled it out or had an accident, or any one of a number of things. He lowered her dress and stood up straight. She was asleep, which was perfect. Eduardo moved to her closet quietly and pulled it open, smiling at the large storage box tucked just behind the door. He glanced over his shoulder and made sure she was still asleep before popping the box open and looking inside. Clothes. Lots of ugly khaki brown clothes. He pushed them aside. Underneath was an old faded black and white photo of Ms. Detmold when she was younger, standing next to a man in a black uniform. Eduardo looked at the picture for a long time, trying to see if he recognized the man, if he was one of the withered husks of a human in one of the many beds here at St. Catherina's Nursing Home. So many of them had come here to Argentina when that war petered out. Finally he put the picture aside and was confronted by a mass of red cloth. A flag. It was old, but soft. It had probably sat here neatly folded since the '40s.

Eduardo set that aside too; it would be worth something on eBay for sure.

Under the flag there was a box. It was about the size of a cigar box. It was covered in chipped black paint with small symbols carved in the wood. He couldn't tell if they were in some other language or just decorative. Most of the text, or scribbles, was obscured by thick wax of different colors. It looked like over the years different candles had been melted on top of the box, allowing the wax to run down and coat it. Eduardo gave the box a gentle shake and winced as he heard the sound of something clattering inside. He looked over at the woman. She was still asleep. This was promising. The box could contain diamonds, or gold, jewelry. Enough of it and he could leave behind this shit job of watching these old fucks die.

Eduardo pulled out his little folding knife and sat on the floor with the box. This late at night the other residential assistants would be asleep in the breakroom or watching Netflix in the office. He worked on the wax seal that held the box shut. After several moments of struggling, he managed to slide the knife under the seal and pry the box open. He peered inside, trying to angle the box to catch the light from the small dim bulb overhead. It flickered. But in that flickering light he could make out dozens, possibly hundreds of white and yellow objects. He lifted one, and with a cry realized what it was, dropping it and the box. The teeth scattered everywhere, clattering and bouncing on the linoleum.

Eduardo turned towards the bed and let out another shout of shock. Ms. Detmold was awake and smiling at him in that way the senile do, where you aren't sure exactly what they are thinking. He wanted to ask her why she kept a box of teeth. He knew she and hers had taken the teeth for the fillings, but these weren't filled with gold. They were just teeth. He wanted to call her creepy, or batty. But nothing came out of his throat. He was choking. Something was lodged in there.

"What is it dear?" Ms. Detmold asked in German, her voice watery and soft, like a muddied creek days away from drying up in the sun.

Eduardo tried to cough, tried to clear his throat, but he couldn't breathe. He felt something sharp and bristled moving in his esophagus. He clawed at his throat, desperate to dislodge whatever was there. All he wanted was to breathe. He looked at the old woman with panicked, begging eyes, but she wasn't moving, not helping, not even seeming to comprehend the pain he was in.

She barely even reacted when the massive segmented leg, like that of a horrifyingly large spider, burst from his throat, showering the room in warm blood. Fingers, pale skinned and blackened with soot, began creeping from his mouth. Two more emerged from his nostrils. His eyes bulged before popping free from his skull, pushed from behind by even more of the stained digits. Still he couldn't scream. His eyeballs, tethered to his skull by the optic nerve, bounced like corpses at the end of a noose as Eduardo spasmed. The thirteen fingers emerging from the various holes in his head wriggled, grasped the edges of his skull, and pulled. With a pop and rip, Edurardo's skull flew apart, adding chunks of skull and quivering masses of gray-pink gelatin to the decor. The fingers were attached to two hands, now revealed, that gripped the sides of Eduardo's ruined skull and pulled, ripping the dead man's body apart and revealing the parasitic creature inside.

It was taller than Eduardo, but painfully thin. Sharp angular bones could easily be seen under the skin. Like a frame of glass fused together with tortured leather stretched over it. It was roughly human. If you ignored the soot stained hands with too many fingers, or the 13 pairs of giant chitinous insect limbs that jutted from its back. The face was feminine, gentle and kind, until you reached the eyes. The eyes were empty holes emitting a strange light that hurt to look at. The air writhed like there were faces pushing into the world from somewhere beyond, trying to get free, trying to get a warning to the other side. The figure wore a simple dress, white and tattered and stained with ash, soot, and blood. She looked at Ms. Demold and clucked her tongue before moving forward.

JOSHUA WAS in Thorsten Friedberg's room when the screaming started. Thorsten was an asshole. He had been some important captain or commander during the war. Before all these Germans had fled like rats fleeing a sinking ship and set up shop in Argentina. Not that it mattered. In the end, time caught up with everyone. Joshua had been helping Mr. Friedberg take his last pills of the day—always an ordeal with the man—when the screams echoed through the hallway. Joshua jumped up startled and then looked down as Friedman started laughing at him.

"You are a coward and a woman," Friedman muttered in German. *"Weak."* How was it they had spent most of their lives in Argentina and never even bothered to learn the language?

"Eduardo will take care of it," Joshua answered in Spanish, still trying to get the old man to just hold the damn pills as he raised the bed into a sitting position.

"Don't talk to me in your mongrel language, you dog," the old man hissed through clenched teeth. It was always the same: the racism, the hatred, the insults. *"And your Eduardo may be brave, but he's a fool and a thief."* That last was said with a sly grin.

Joshua rolled his eyes. The residents were always accusing someone of stealing something. It was inevitable at their age they forgot what they owned, forgot where they were. The paranoia they had come with was only growing more acute. "I'm sure he isn't robbin…"

Another scream cut him off, this one almost more of a wail. Joshua looked up, biting his lip. "Ok, I should check on that." He set Thorsten's pills on the nightstand next to the table and glanced down at the horrible old man. *"If you try to hide those, I'll find them. Just wait for me to come back to take them."*

HE LEFT the room and jogged down the hallway. St. Catherina's was not a massive facility, but it wasn't tiny either. Housing just under forty residents, all German immigrants, the place was large enough to be spacious without being sprawling. The money the Germans had brought when they came here had been enough to set them on an easy path of government bribery and comfort. Joshua rounded the corner, looking for the source of the screams. But everything was quiet now.

In the darkened hallway the only sounds came from his tennis shoes on the linoleum, the rasp of respirators, and the occasional beep of some life support machine. He paused, not sure where the hell he was running to. The screaming had stopped, but he wasn't sure if that was a comfort or not. Joshua knew something was wrong. He could feel it in his stomach, like a sour note that was slowly expanding and turning in unnatural angles inside him. The easiest way to do this was to just check on everyone. Check each and every room to ensure that all the residents were unhurt and still alive.

Joshua walked—calmer now that there was no one actively screaming—to the last room in the hallway, Mrs. Detmold's, and opened the door. The light was off. But the smell in the room was suffocating. Like someone had smeared rotten eggs and shit all over the walls. For a moment, Joshua thought about just closing the door, letting the old bat marinate in her juices. It wouldn't be the first time she had smeared feces everywhere. Mostly, he admitted, he didn't want to risk touching her shit if it was on the light switch. He started to close the door but stopped himself. If he didn't clean it now, it would harden and be even more difficult to clean later. And he was sure the morning manager would make him clean it before he could leave. Cursing to himself, he reached in, and flicked on the light.

To his credit, he didn't scream. Though that was less due to bravery and more to the way the gory scene robbed him of the ability to say or do anything. The walls looked like a bomb filled with blood, shit, and viscera had gone off in the room. A bomb that had been comprised primarily of Eduardo. His skin lay like discarded clothes after someone had fallen into the lake, all wrinkled and boneless. His dead eyes sat on opposite ends of the room, trailing the ocular cord to what was left of his ruined face. Joshua assumed it was his face. There was no skull to give it shape, and it was ripped in half like a plastic bag that had held something too large and too sharp. Sitting in the mess of Eduardo was a small cigar box filled with glistening teeth.

But that wasn't the worst thing. What was left of Mrs. Detmold was far worse. She had been peeled. Her skeleton was intact, most of it still laying in the hospital bed. But her muscles, organs and … well, everything else was suspended above her bed from small hooks that had been attached to the ceiling. Her nerve endings had been pulled out and tied around the hooks in her flesh, allowing whoever had done this to play with her pain like a harpsichord. Half of her skull was ripped open, and her brain sat in the basin. Every tooth had been wrenched from her jaw. Her eyes, still wedged in the shrunken muscles of her skinned face, swiveled madly, coming loose and falling down onto the bed. She couldn't make a noise. She shouldn't be alive. Joshua stepped back into the hallway. His mind reeling, unable to process the sheer magnitude of suffering and violence he had witnessed. He heard a whimper behind him, from an open door.

Mr. Trenik! Joshua crossed the hallway as quickly as he could force his body to move. He didn't want to see what had done that to Mrs. Detmold. But he couldn't just leave the old man on his own. He stopped in the doorway. The light was off in here too. Joshua snaked an arm in to turn on the light and froze when he heard a voice.

"*Ah Geoffrey.*" The voice was like spiders skittering across glass shards that were being dragged across a chalkboard. They carved rivulets of pain through his mind and brought his gorge to his throat. It spoke in horrible rasping German. "*We were denied our dance, so many years ago.*"

Geoff Trenik whimpered in the darkness. Mr. Trenik had always been a kind and patient man. It had always been a mystery what he had done during the war. How could such a kind man be part of the German war machine? Joshua's fingers hovered near the lights, terror paralyzing him. It wasn't until the screams started that Joshua was able to move. Part of him hoped that, as he flicked on the switch, it would all prove to be a dream. A hallucination brought on by smoking too much pot before coming to work with the elderly. After all, he could have just fallen asleep in the office.

The light did not banish the nightmare. It stood there. A woman that was as much spider as human, whose body was starved and stretched and jutted at painfully wrong angles. She was staring at Joshua, staring at him even as she dug her hands under Mr. Trenik's ribs to take hold of his withered lungs and shred at them with too many too sharp fingers. The dark holes where she should have been keeping her eyes were locked on him.

"Don't worry little sweety, I'll be with you shortly," it promised in Spanish this time, and then turned its horrible empty sockets back to Mr. Trenik. The thing wrenched his bottom ribs out of his chest with a sickening crack. Joshua turned to run, but his guts twisted at the sounds and smells and forced him to his knees to vomit. He emptied his stomach, his mind focused in animal fear on trying to get up and move the entire time. It was going to get him if he stayed here, it was going to get him.

"I'm going to get you no matter where you run." The spiders-on-glass voice whispered in his ear.

Joshua bolted, rising then slipping and stumbling through his own vomit. His feet scrambled on the tile made slick with his sick as he tumbled through the hallway towards the front doors. The noise brought out Sandra, the third and final member of the night crew. She watched Joshua running and stepped out of his way as he rushed past her and grabbed the handle of the front door, yanking it with all of his might.

It didn't open.

It was locked. Of course it was locked. They locked it to make sure none of the residents got out and wandered off in a dementia-fueled fugue. He could have laughed if his mind wasn't still reeling from terror. He unlocked the door and yanked again.

It didn't open.

"Josh? What's going on?" Sandra asked sleepily. She had probably dozed off in the office. Josh had a terrible crush on Sandra, who was a sturdy girl, strong, the kind of bitch no one wanted to mess with. But she wore tight clothes that sometimes showed more skin than normal, and Joshua had become smitten, though he was too shy to ask to see her outside work.

"We have to get out of here, it's coming!" He needed to save her, to play the hero.

He turned to look back at her, and behind her he saw the hallway lights flickering. They were turning off, the bulbs quietly dying one by one, plunging the back of the nursing home into a horrible blackness. Within the dark, something moved from room to room.

"Oh fuck oh fuck oh fuck," Joshua said and threw himself against the door.

Sandra was about to ask him what the hell was going on when another scream echoed through the building. "What the fuck?" Sandra yelped, turning towards the hallway, trying to see into the shadows. "Is Eduardo doing that? Is he doing something?"

Josh didn't answer, instead moving to the big reception desk, looking for something, anything he could use as a weapon. Sandra gave up on getting an answer from Joshua. Eduardo was a punk ass. Oh sure, he was cute enough, but other than occasionally getting and giving head in the office on slow nights, she didn't have much patience with him. She marched down the hallway to see what he was doing to hurt the old assholes. Joshua watched her go before turning back to find the gun he knew was stashed in one of these drawers. If he didn't move fast he would never get to ask Sandra out. He had to save her. It took him several minutes to check all the drawers, and finally he found the old .33 they kept on hand for emergencies. He turned towards the hallway. Sandra came dashing out of the darkness towards him. Or parts of her did.

Sandra's jaw had been ripped off. Drool-infused strands of dark red blood dripped in long thick ropes from the wound. Her tongue lolled about with no bottom jaw, and the soot stained fingers of the horrible woman pushed through the back of Sandra's skull and through her eye sockets. The orbs bounced and dangled as the horrible woman used Sandra's corpse as a puppet.

She spoke in a falsetto which screeched against Joshua's brain, migraines exploded behind his eyes. "What is it Joshy? Don't you still want me to suck your cock? Hmmm? Too long wishing you were Eduardo, too little action."

She bounced the body about as she approached him. Joshua raised the gun but couldn't shoot into Sandra's body. The chitin-covered limbs carried the woman forward silently, as though she were gliding through the air. Sandra's body convulsed. She was still alive! Sandra could see the floor moving under her. She could feel the too-long, too many jointed, too many fingers caressing her brain and guiding her body. The pain was like nothing she had ever imagined. She wanted to scream but she couldn't draw enough air to do so. She was in a race with her own body to discover if lack of blood or oxygen would kill her first.

She would never find out. The creature twisted her hand, clenching her fingers into a fist, crushing skull to powder and pulping the brain which ran through her fingers. Sandra's mutilated and convulsing body fell to the floor, letting the last electrical impulses of a savaged brain pulse pain throughout every nerve ending.

The woman-thing stood there, head tilted as it watched Joshua waving his gun at her. The hand still dripping with gore and brains was raised in the air. Slowly the woman opened her fingers again, revealing a cigar box covered in black paint and old dried wax. "Almost full, but no matter, there is always room for more." She glided forward.

Joshua fired. The bullet went wide. He hadn't discharged a gun before. He screamed and squeezed the trigger several more times, missing every shot. The woman almost looked surprised, the eyebrows above her empty sockets raised in cruel mockery of his ineptitude.

"Why?" He screamed. "Why are you doing this?"

To Josh's terrified surprise, she answered him. "I was summoned in Oświęcim, tasked with setting things right, setting these Germans to task ... and before I could finish my work." She looked down at the box filled with teeth. "Before I could finish my work, I was impris-oned. A trophy, a thing to be kept while they kept to their own grisly work."

Josh realized that this creature must have been some sort of Jewish demon, summoned during the war. "That was so long ago, all of the people you were defending are gone now, and all these Germans are harmless. They are old."

"No, they are dead," she corrected, smiling sweetly, and it was the most horrifying and cruel thing he had seen in his entire short life.

"Then it's done ... you can leave, you can let me leave ... please..." he whimpered.

"No, it's not done." She spat at him. "Their kind flourish, feeding on the inaction and the apathy of those around them. You knew what they were." She seemed to grow, filling the hall with shadows and pallid skin. Skittering things filled the gloom behind her as she swelled to fill his vision. "You showed them kindness and succor. There can be no redemption, no mercy. I will fill this box with the teeth of all who have aided them, and Joshua..." Her face was directly in front of him. He could feel her hand on his cheek, her chitinous limbs surrounding him in a spider's embrace. "There is always room for more."

LUTZNAU'S OPUS
BY JONATHAN LOUIS DUCKWORTH

Berlin, German Reich, 1944

Good morning, brave inspectors of the Gestapo, I hope the walk up to the fifth floor wasn't too taxing. The handyman who used to repair the elevator was conscripted and sent to the Eastern Front in May. I imagine he's dead by now. I wonder, who will be conscripted to replace him? The black-marketeer baker on the second floor? Herr Scharr upstairs who dances waltzes by himself? One of you?

If you're trying to speak with me, or to coerce me into unlocking the vault, I'm afraid I can't hear you. Our communication is strictly one-way, which is just as well, as I doubt you'd have anything of interest to tell me. You are disappointed, aren't you? You've found me, Rachel Lutznau, perhaps the last free Jewess in Berlin, and I have the temerity to delay the inevitable by hiding within a steel vault built into the walls of my apartment. This was once the flat of the great film-maker, Klaus Lutznau, my brother. He built the vault to preserve his films and his other prized possessions. The door is made from Krupp steel, the same as casts the barrels of your Wehrmacht's artillery. You are no doubt sending for a safecracker now, and when he arrives, I'm certain he will be impressed by the workmanship of the vault's mechanism.

I knew the alias of Bernadette Meinhoff would crumble against scrutiny. It was always a matter of time before someone found discrepancies in the records, and before those discrepancies summoned men such as yourselves to my threshold. Where will you send me once you've broken in? Will I be sent to Poland or Ukraine, or to a camp within the Reich? Perhaps you will spare me the formality of a train ride and find a way to pump gas into this vault. Oh, it must be so terribly oppressive to have a Jew in your midst. I do sympathize, truly.

Since you are a captive audience, why don't I tell you a story? It's what we old ladies love most, to talk the ears off strapping young men like yourselves. By now, you've probably already destroyed the speaker, and you've noticed that my voice still finds its way to your ears. Wonderful, isn't it?

I was born here in the Kreuzberg District. It was 1877, and Berlin was such a spectacularly filthy place in those days. I imagine there was coal dust even in Mother's womb. Mother was a seamstress of Russian extraction, Father a laborer of old Berliner stock. I remember them as tired ghosts whenever they were there at all. Little Klaus was born in '92 when I was already most of the way to womanhood. Between our births was a long string of fizzles, so many miscarriages that when Klaus finally survived to term and emerged into the world, it was the closest thing our family had ever known to a miracle. But miracles are brief things; burdens live and grow.

Is it cruel to call a brother a burden? Should I be kinder to the dead?

We were never siblings. Siblings grow up together, and I was grown by the time he spoke his first word. Many years later, Klaus would tell lies about how his own sister nursed him with the milk of her teat. Isn't that obscene? Even men such as yourselves must think so.

Both of us were afflicted with pretensions of artistry, as well as by a greater curse: talent. I was fated for the seamstress's life, while Klaus was destined to follow Father into the sooty lung of the boot

factory. And yet from an early age I knew I wanted to be an artist—a
painter. I had no money for paints or canvases, but I was resourceful. I
made my own pigments from whatever I could scrounge, used scraps
of cloth from my mother's trade as surfaces, and crafted my own
brushes from used toothbrushes. Mother mocked my dream, and
Father behaved as if my artistic endeavors were some embarrassing
hysteria. But I persisted. I had a prized possession, a book of the
painter Bernadette Bornholm's works. How acutely she captured the
sorrow of the human condition in her portraiture of inbred nobles and
ignorant rustics.

When I was eighteen—Klaus was only three—I learned that Frau
Bernadette still lived in an old house near Flensburg. I learned her
address, and sent her letters, paying for the postage through rather
indiscreet means. Can you imagine the unearthly shock when I
received a reply from her, and a request that I share my own work? I
no longer have our correspondence, but the physical letters are less
important than the knowledge she imparted to me. Lessons I would
share with Klaus, though he never understood them as well as I did.
Frau Bernadette taught me that art was the most supreme force of
transposition and translocation, and it is through art that we may
transport the self to other realms of sublimity and terror.

Is your Führer not an artist himself, albeit a failed one? I wonder
how different our world would look if he had possessed any sense of
perspective, and I mean that in all the word's meanings.

Frau Bernadette died just before the Great War, and I never had the
chance to meet her in person, for though she had invited me to visit,
her home near the Danish border might as well have been on the
moon. She took to her grave a wealth of knowledge: of painting, but of
other things too, for she was a student of the esoteric and the Old
Science of the Dark. She passed to me a trickle of the wisdom she
gleaned from the great Fabian Kastl, himself merely a modern eaves-
dropper to antediluvian secrets.

Do you like the paintings hanging from the walls of the parlor?
They are my work. The gloomy portrait hanging near the door to the
kitchen is one of my early works—that is Klaus, as painted following

his return from the Western Front. You will note his distended ears, vast forehead, nonexistent chin, translucent lips, and crooked nose. Jew features, you will notion. Notice how his eyes, in an inversion of that cliché about old portraits, avoid yours? He never could look anyone in the eye; like me, he always saw too much.

Klaus discovered his own artistic gifts from a young age. He was drawn not to the arcane wiles of the canvas but to her young and fashionable cousin: photography. In sheets of tin and squares of silver-bromide the living world was being imprisoned and immortalized in fragments. But there is a certain irony in the durability of a photograph's image measured against the fragility of the substance upon which it is developed. Is it not like taking an immortal, inviolate soul and sewing it into a cask of flesh that is already putrefying the instant it emerges into being?

Has the safecracker arrived yet with his tools and his stethoscope? Is he suffering terribly from my prattle? Oh, I do sympathize. Tell me, Safecracker, do you hear something other than my voice? Do you hear, perhaps, the click of a spinning reel? The warm crackle of an old phonograph, a whisper of music?

When Klaus was fifteen—the same year my mentor Bernadette died—, he earned his first job, not in the boot factory as we'd all expected, but as a photographer for the police. It paid almost nothing, but he was able to pursue his passion for gainful employment in a way I never could. Klaus took unflinching photographs of cadavers, mugshots of surly career criminals—subjects that would serve as inspiration in his later cinematic exploits.

Then the Great War happened. Like so many young men, Klaus was conscripted and sent to fight for the Fatherland, which had taken as good care of us as our actual Father had. I'd like to tell you Klaus was brave, earning medals for his valor and so on, but the truth is, Klaus shat in a trench in Flanders and sat in the shit for three years waiting to die.

Sometimes letters arrived from the front. Klaus would speak of how he missed me. Auntie, he'd always call me in his letters, *Auntie*

Rachel, how I've missed your touch, your smell. Will you kiss me again when I am home?

Does that unsettle you?

And what of your poor, frustrated safecracker? Does the mechanism seem to you impossible? Does it seem, each time you think you have discerned its solution, that there are yet more complexities frustrating your ingress? Do you suspect the mechanism is a sentient chaos, scornful of your attempts to solve it? Perhaps you can ring your office for a kerosene torch, or even dynamite.

Listen. Where has the noise of the cars on the streets gone? What do you make of Berlin's sudden silence?

In October of 1917, Klaus's trench was struck by mustard gas. Some fifty men died and nearly three hundred more were sent to field hospitals, covered in bleeding pustules and blind in many cases. As for Klaus, he was reported missing. His body was not among the dead after the gas attack, but no one could find him, and his regiment assumed he had deserted, or perhaps—blinded and delirious from the gas—run across No-man's-land to his death.

Almost a month later, the men of Klaus's company were repairing the trench after a shelling when a soldier's shovel uncovered a hollow, at first assumed to be an old rabbit warren. That theory was quickly abandoned when the men excavated the hollow and found it to be so expansive that the light of their lanterns barely touched the bottom. What they had found was a crack in the world, a thing you will not find written of in any reputable geological study, but which I can assure you from my own studies are quite commonplace, if you have the knowledge to find them, as I do and Klaus did. To escape the mustard gas, Klaus had crawled through a seam of the earth into another place entirely, and there he had gotten himself stuck for a month.

He was, of course, famished and near to dying of thirst, but, as the army physicians asserted, he shouldn't have been alive at all after a month without food or water. He was a living spindle, his hair now drained of color and brittle as dry straw. The other soldiers and the doctors who tended him noted the semi-translucence of his skin—not only were his every vein and capillary visible, but so too were distinct muscle fibers observable through the diaphanous sheen of his dermis, such that he might have been redeployed to a medical school to serve as a living anatomical model. When doctors felt for his pulse, it came in irregular but not entirely random bursts. Like Morse Code, one doctor noted. Klaus refused to tell anyone in the army what he had seen, and insisted he had no memory of what had transpired while he was in the hole, and perhaps that was true. Before they collapsed the hollow, a soldier of Klaus's company explored its interior, and reported that the walls of the cavern bore the impressions of what looked like claws of burrowing animals.

With time the opacity returned to Klaus's skin and he managed to regain a semblance of healthy bodyweight, but his hair stayed white and brittle until it fell off altogether. After his medical discharge, Klaus returned to Berlin to live with me and our parents, who both caught influenza and died the following year. It wasn't a very important tragedy, but still worth noting.

Klaus returned to photography. The war ended, Germany became a Republic, and a new epoch began, one where artists like Klaus and I were no longer scorned as useless eccentrics but were instead celebrated by the new zeitgeist of Expressionism.

Klaus began his career in cinema as a cameraman, but his rare, intuitive talent for composition earned him the attention of certain important figures in studios long since shuttered by your Party. These men gave him the opportunity to direct his own films. His earliest works were technically competent if uninspired. Crime capers, maudlin romances: crowd-pleasing nonsense, you know. But it didn't take long for my brother to find his niche with the genre of the grotesque and the terrifying.

Many of his more celebrated works of horror have been outlawed by the Reich Chamber of Culture, destroyed as "decadent Jewish filth." But I preserved as many of his reels as I could. Perhaps you saw some of them in theaters when you were schoolboys. Do you remember *The Sea Emperor?* It was a batty little picture about a lighthouse keeper in the Baltic who goes mad thinking that Neptune is calling him to the sea. In an interview regarding *The Sea Emperor*, Klaus told a newspaperman that his intent with his films was for audiences to feel transported. That they would leave the theaters wondering if they were walking in the same world as before, and that they would reach out into the night and feel the moist lining of the alien stomach now digesting them.

Do you remember the backdrops? I painted those, just as I designed and painted most of the scenery in Klaus's films, designs that were imitated by other, more successful contemporaries—you know the ones: Murnau, Lang, Wiene, et al. Klaus fell in with that lot, although I don't know that "friendship" is what I would call their associations. Truer to say he was their pet madman. Klaus was, even at his best, known as a deviant among deviants. Even Murnau, known to all as an invert, thought Klaus an odd duck. Still, he was their peer, and though they all whispered scandalous gossip about him blinding an assistant with acid (completely false) or exposing himself to one of his actresses on set (unfortunately true), they were also jealous of his work.

Has the torch arrived yet, or have you resolved to blow up the flat to get at me? Are you running out of patience? I do sympathize. Look out the window; what color is the sun now? Is there a sun?

As the Twenties fizzled against economic ruin, many suspected Klaus to be a morphine addict, but it was not a needle that gnawed at him. You see, gentlemen, you can never simply open a crack in the world without it opening something in you. When he escaped into the world beneath—or perhaps more appropriately, *parallel* to—our own, a trickle of that dark world leaked into him.

His neuroses—incessant fidgeting, unprovoked tirades against cast and crew, his habit of disappearing for days at a time—worsened, and the films he made became stranger and more unsettling to the point they no longer entertained, for much as we might inject ourselves with the dormant residue of the diphtheria toxin to inure ourselves to that disease, we seek an inert horror in our cinema. One to inoculate us against the real terror our world conceals in its closed fist, and that men like your Führer have revealed.

It was that true, unmarketable horror that Klaus's newer films exposited, and for this he was abandoned by the studios of Germany. Nor would any studio in America think of offering him work as they had to some of his peers. At the same time, your kind were propagating like a squamous clump on the skin of the nation, and working your way into its bloodstream. Klaus and I watched the violence in the streets and the steady rise of your Party and your Führer with what you might call morbid fascination. I regret my insouciance now, but at the time I thought you were the most ridiculous, sad little men I'd ever seen, with your silly brown shirts and your garish Hackenkreuze and your insipid rhetoric of Übermensch and Untermenschen.

In 1932, the year before your Party seized absolute power, Klaus produced what would be his final film, entitled *Three Short Horrors*. It was a film of three vignettes. Without a studio to bankroll it, and his name and credit in tatters, Klaus bankrupted himself to fund it, hiring amateurs for his cast and workmen with no experience in the industry for his crew.

The film was never released to a broad audience, and for that I am grateful. As it was, it did more damage than I could have anticipated, even knowing the forces I'd taught Klaus to summon.

Although the broader public never saw Klaus's opus, he did hold private screenings for that small coterie of bohemians who still admired him. October 1932, the month his film was completed, was the same month that Berlin experienced a strange rash of disappearances and an equally unaccountable string of suicides. Unaccountable to press and public, but not to me.

It is the suicides you may recall from newspapers, as they were sensational. More than twenty people in the space of three weeks: struggling actors and actresses, amateur cameramen, destitute carpenters, and various unskilled laborers who shared one thing in common: they had worked on the production of Klaus's film. Apart from that, there was one other commonality in the suicides: that no matter what the actual method of self-termination was, every victim displayed the same medically inexplicable affliction: their eyes were bleached white, and their bodies dotted with purulent sores war veterans would recognize as symptomatic of mustard gas exposure.

Then there were the disappearances. Dozens of people vanished over the same period of time. No evidence of abduction, no sign that they fled somewhere. The disappeared people were all artists, bohemians, aesthetes, and radicals: Klaus's most steadfast patrons and enthusiasts, and all those who had attended screenings with him.

Klaus was sought out by the police, who brought him in for questioning, but what could they have hoped to prove? I believe, burdened by guilt, he may have told them the truth, and it was for that reason that my brother was at last committed to a sanitarium, where he spent the last months of his unhappy time on this world. I visited him there once in the spring of 1933, and I found him lucid, more sound of mind and body than he had been since before the war. He had warned his whitecoated wardens of what was coming for him, but they didn't listen, only saw it as more evidence of his psychosis.

Klaus Lutznau disappeared from the world for the second and last time in August of 1933, and this time the crack through which he'd slipped was too fine for any shovel to find.

Now then. Aren't you curious what Klaus's film *was*? I can tell you, for I have seen it.

As I said there are three vignettes, and the first is entitled "The Maggot."

As the reel begins to spin, we see a backdrop of a forest. Dark, skinny trees with bare branches the shape of deer's antlers. Against this grim and barren vista, a paleness resolves itself. What is this bloated, white thing we see? Is it a dead whale? Is it a mountain of pale lard?

No. It's a maggot, as you might find devouring dead birds or rotting dog carcasses or the eyes of babies in train cars. An enormous maggot that—were it a real thing—would rival in size the tallest of Berlin's buildings. The score that plays is a simple melody, strings harsh as the creak of a rusted door hinge, a piano that progresses through an inane adagio in B-minor. The camera closes in on the pallid, gelatinous bulk of the maggot, and we see fissures along the flank, and from these embrasures emerge what look like people. And we wonder: are these full-sized people emerging from the corpse of a giant maggot, or are they microscopic gnomes that scavenge the larvae that infest our own remains, their debauched feasts unnoticed by our undiscerning eyes? These things that look like people take fistfuls of the putrid meat, and the camera is almost shy to their feasting, except for when it lingers on a single subject, one of the last of the gnomic larvaphages to emerge: a woman, naked like the others, with a Paleolithic tangle of black hair framing her white face. She alone shows discomfort, but like the others she eats the meat on hand. This woman—or the actress who portrays her—happens to bear an uncanny resemblance to the director's sister in her younger years.

The next vignette is entitled "The Bathroom."

This piece is without score, and it is pervaded by a sterile silence as we might imagine holds sway on the barren, nighted steppes of the moon. The establishing shot is the bowl of a porcelain bathtub. There is a drain, and around this drain a ring of black algae has accreted, while at the rim of the hole are long coils and strands of black hair. The scene changes, we see the bathroom in the totality of its banal emptiness. There is a medicine cabinet with a cracked mirror. There is the tub we saw before—one of the old clawfooted ones common in the last century, but this is of the cheaper sort with dull pewter appendages.

And then the woman appears, quite *ex nihilo*. Stark naked, naturally. She is there and we wonder if she was always there and if we only noticed her staring at us now. We recognize her as the same woman from the first vignette, although she looks older now, and skinnier, as if her feasting stole more sustenance than it gave. We see the shadow and light of her ribs like piano keys. She stares, her arms slack at her side, her eyes never blinking. And while she stands immobile, we notice subtle movement from inside the bathtub. Threads of black begin to writhe, thin and imperceptible as spiderline at first, but as they coalesce and braid, they become oily damp tendrils, and these tendrils merge into a thick rope, and this rope resolves itself into the shape of a noose. The woman is oblivious to the terror amassing behind her. Maybe she is as deaf as we are. It snakes toward her, rising, the noose's loop falling over her head, and now we know—if we did not recognize it sooner—that is the same material as her own hair, the assembled sheddings of a thousand ablutions made animate. The noose shimmers as it cinches around the woman's throat. She does not resist as her own hair drags her inexorably headfirst into the tub. We see her limbs sprawled, we see her body folded by a sudden, violent tug. Then the limbs break as ever greater force drags her down into the drain. With sufficient will and power, a camel can be dragged through the eye of a needle. And that is all.

You are by this point, I imagine, quite at a loss for words. The torch isn't working, is it? Whatever scant discoloration the heat paints on the steel, there is no real damage. You may find yourself taking a closer look at the vault. It is not the smooth, unblemished finish of Krupp steel. You're asking yourselves: does it resemble the grain of animal muscle? Was this hulk of metal alive once? Is it alive now? Look, the windows are black.

But now, I still must tell you of the final piece, entitled "Three Blind Mice."

For its score, we have an odd rendition of the nursery rhyme of the same name. It is not offkey so much as mistimed, and the ear can't help but fixate on how the intervals between notes is always a touch too long. We are so distracted by this that we barely notice the banal setting of the piece, nor its equally dreary players. Three middle-aged men sit at a café table. The backdrop is a city scene, an anonymous neighborhood in Berlin, ordinary, except that there are plumes of black smoke arising from some of the buildings, and the longer we stare, the more it seems those plumes of painted smoke are wafting against their stilllife backdrop.

Dialogue cards relay to us the men's conversation. But it's not really a conversation, as only one of the men is talking. This one looks familiar to us, somehow. Perhaps this passing resemblance is in his jawline, or in his nose and eyes, or perhaps in the postage stamp of hair on his upper lip. We know this man, for his face is everywhere now.

He is telling the other men a story. Recently he suffered a rat infestation in his home. Always the rodents kept him up nights with their incessant scurrying, and distracted him whenever he tried to paint. Then one day, he tells them, he had enough and bought poison and an aerosol dispenser to pump the poison into the crawlspace where the rodents lived. He did so, and the rodents, blind and choking on the poison, a whole damn family of the vermin—came scurrying out into his home, bloody sores erupting from their bodies. Further enraged at the sight of these dying rats, the man got a hammer and smashed them to pulp, until he could no longer tell what they had once been.

As he talks, we notice that the café window behind the men, black and opaque, becomes less opaque, and we see the Woman's pale face emerge from the black. Wide-eyed and gaunter than before. She presses a hand to the glass. She is—there is no other word for it: she is skeletal. Her hair has been shaved, leaving a withered, dry scalp patched with stubble and scars. The man has continued talking all the while, though we don't know what he was saying, and really it doesn't matter. Suddenly, the three men look directly at the camera. They have noticed the glass eye. They have noticed *us*. But as they regard their audience with blank incomprehension, they fail to notice the things perched upon the awning above their heads.

These things are shaped like men, but their oily black bodies terminate in broad, clawed shovel-like feet such as moles have, and their heads are long, spindly, and eyeless. But they can smell the men beneath them; we are sure they can. And there the film ends.

Have you given up yet? Is your safecracker still trying to solve the fustian riddle of the lock? Is his stethoscope pressed to the steel? If so, does he notice the faint susurrus of a spinning film reel has ceased, and that no longer do his ears suffer the rumor of a mistimed rendition of "Three Blind Mice" on piano?

Brave inspectors of the Gestapo, let me be honest now. I am not in this vault. I am not in Berlin at all, nor indeed anywhere in the world you know. And now, neither are any of you.

Look around. Does it now occur to you that all pigment has drained from the room? That the paintings once grotesque with color are now studies in gray? Does the very air you breathe taste ammoniac? You didn't notice these changes as you toiled to get at me. You are lobsters set into a cold pot of water slowly heated to boiling, that don't know they're dying until their nervous systems are steam and gelatin.

It is not necessary to *see* Klaus's film. Its mere presence is enough to transport you—its presence, and an understanding of its contents, which I have given to you. Words to the ear are as good as light to the eye. When you leave this apartment and step out into the street, you won't recognize the buildings that arch and twist in impossible dimensions. To even look at them will drive you to vertigo.

Are you frightened? I do sympathize.

The creatures who call this world home—they who tunnel beneath ours and sometimes make cracks in its foundation—they will be hungry. And by now they will have already smelled you.

For what happened to my brother, I am sorry. Much as I am sorry for all the innocent people who his film—our film—destroyed. But to you? I only wish I could have trapped more of you swine.

Do you feel it now?

Can you feel the wet, fever-hot inner lining of the stomach digesting you?

BRIDE OF THE WHITE RAT
BY JOE KOCH

The cage fits Kyle's face like the one from the Orwell story. He made it himself after stealing the book from the library. Sam's nervous about the thing. Usually she agrees with her man, but when he said to starve the rats, Sam didn't have the heart to watch them suffer. She's been sneaking Cheetos and hamburger on the sly.

"I swear, if you've been feeding them," Kyle says.

Sam giggles at the threat. She does that when she's edgy. "I'm sorry, you sound funny. I can't help it if they're sweet on you."

The cage is strapped onto Kyle's face with three belts and two metal clamps. It looks like homemade armor for an elaborate Halloween costume. Instead of a single helmet, it has double compartments: one encases Kyle's head, and one sticks out perpendicular from his face to hold rats.

Billy the rat is in the extension. He's Sam's favorite. She's just raised the faceplate dividing the compartments as Kyle instructed. Not only is Billy nuzzling, interfering with Kyle's ability to speak, but the apparatus itself presses Kyle's jaw in such a way that his pronunciation is fucked up.

Kyle sits straight-backed in a reclaimed office chair in the middle of the small kitchen, gripping the arms with bulging knuckles. He figures if rats eating your face is the worst the libs can think up, he's going to be ready for them when the torture starts. Kyle's smart. He'll beat them at their own game before they come for him.

"Ahhhh!" he yells at the docile and confused Billy. "Come on, motherfucker!"

Kyle doesn't listen when Sam suggests he's going too far. Kyle reminds her about discipline, and how he's doing this for her as much as him. Of course Sam doesn't admit she pampers the rats behind Kyle's back, pulls them out of their cages and cuddles when he's out. Billy's used to human smooches. He bops Kyle's nose and turns in circles, seeking treats.

Kyle shakes in the chair, growling out a challenge. He's a sick vocalist. His band is going places. Sam wants him to be happy, wants to be true to the cause, but some of the shit he's been pulling lately is making her paranoid. She's not blind. She can see the country going down the toilet, how hard it is for two people to get by on her paycheck alone, how the younger customers sneer if you say so much as Merry Christmas. But the poor little rats never hurt anyone.

Billy's puffing up now, trapped in the cage on Kyle's face. Sam grabs Kyle's shoulders. She says, "Stop."

Kyle rocks back and forth, impervious to her ministrations. His angry barks are punctuated by panicked squeaks. Billy hisses, a sinister sound that makes Sam's hair stand on end. Claws skitter against metal. Kyle yelps and whips his caged head back and forth. Blood flings out. Kyle squeals, thrashing harder: "Fuck, fuck, fuck!"

Sam grapples with the clamps. Kyle's fists pound the chair. He grabs for the helmet. Blood spatters Sam's hands. They slip. Kyle screams an octave higher than his normal range. Billy squeals until one last piercing screech halts the aural torment.

Loosening the last belt, Sam rips the cage from Kyle's head. Kyle spits out the dead rat. Billy's crunched head drops from between Kyle's bloody teeth. Kyle spits again, bending over the long-tailed corpse with leaking guts and stained white fur.

Billy's little claws keep twitching. Sam bursts into tears.

Kyle whips around and slams Sam into the refrigerator, pinning her by the throat. Sam stops crying because she can't breathe. Kyle's face is pockmarked with scratches and pinhole-sized puncture wounds. His left eyelid is split, and the eye is bloodshot, shining red. His nose looks like the center of a human dartboard. White fur and pink globs hang from his lower lip.

Kyle's eyes are aglow with rage. Sam knows it won't last. She hangs tight as her lungs get that funny feeling of impetuous need. She can handle a little pain. It's usually worth it for the make-up sex later. Sure enough, the wild in Kyle's eyes turns to glee. He grins. Then he shoves her once more and moshes away with a loud laugh.

"Yeah! Motherfucking yeah!"

His dance of triumph gives Sam a chance to run to the sink for a washcloth and open the tap wide to get the water hot. Before Kyle comes grabbing her ass to celebrate, Sam wants that blood off his face and those rat guts out of his mouth.

YOU: brunette, lush, dark. I smell the dirt in your hair. I smell your dead children, your lovers like compost. The smell of a world that's falling apart from mistrust. Falling out of orbit. Not much of a nova; a fizzle, smoke.

There was this dental hygienist. She kept talking about how much she loved her mother's hair, how she loved to touch it, stroke it, and spread it out on a pillow. I couldn't respond because her instruments were in my mouth.

She reminds me of you.

You remind me of a girl I used to know. You remind me of a memory. You say you're sorry in a million ways without saying it. You part your hair different when he gives you shit, and you pretend I'm not going to notice.

You should know better. Our history lives in your hair with the smell of smoke. You can't hide from me, no matter how you part it. Shave your head, and I'll sniff you out by the burnt edges of your stubble.

Rub pinpricks across my lips. The sound of stubble scrapes like a new beard. No one but me is close enough to hear you.

You're my memory now, Sam, and he doesn't know us.

He doesn't know anything about you.

IN NINETEEN SEVENTY-EIGHT, while shooting a new version of Nosferatu, the famous German filmmaker said: "We are a generation without fathers, and we must therefore reach back to the true German heritage." In re-making the vampire classic of pre-war German cinema, he played leap-frog over the Nazi era, effecting an intentional blind spot. American interviewers tried to force a more political conversation because many veterans of the war and survivors of the holocaust were still alive at the time. They had experienced the effects of a fascist government first hand. The filmmaker resisted confrontation, and contextualized his film only according to his country's tradition of art.

Human memory is short. During the century that popularized fascism, the filmmaker chose to call a vampire film his most "culturally authentic" work. A correlation between vampires and plague seems blatant enough in viewing, but the full cultural or political message of the film remains garbled, if such a message exists.

In investigating the film, the director's intentions and the fictional melodrama on screen are far less horrific than the shocking behind-the-scenes facts about the terrible fate of thousands of rats.

TEN DAYS after his multiple rat bites, Kyle's face has transformed from injured to healing to horrific. His initial scabs are gone, replaced by red spots that look as innocuous as acne at first. Sam notices his skin feels warmer. It stretches taut with internal pressure. She can hardly look at it, the way it seeps from a ruddy pink tone to greenish-purple, like bruises painted in watercolor. Kyle's left eye is swollen half shut. The broken lid looks like a miniature black hole up close, as if someone bored a pencil into the crease where lid and eyeball and socket intersect. Lead-colored vining spreads from the hole to his surrounding skin.

Sam hoped Kyle would chill out after the rats. The last thing Sam wants to do is go back to her mom's with her tail between her legs. Sam reminds herself how much she craves Kyle's intensity. It's what made her fall in love with him.

He says, "Look at me. Point your finger and laugh."

His fists are clenched, swaying by his sides. Kyle can never keep still. Sam used to find it cute, but right now it makes her heart drop down into her stomach. Add Kyle's discomfort in the ill-fitting dress, his anxiety about wearing women's clothing, and Sam can't even manage her usual involuntary giggle. Sam opens wide and forces air out of her mouth. "Ha."

The familiar dress isn't helping Sam perform, with its tiny red flowers and frumpy green velvet collar. When Kyle told Sam to steal a dress from her mom's big enough to fit him, the Christmas formal was fancy and outdated enough to be stuck in the back of the closet. It wouldn't be noticed, at least not right away. Lucky for Sam, Mom hasn't said anything. But then, Sam's mom never said much about anything, except never trust what comes out of any man's lousy mouth. That they're all the same.

Sam can prove her mom wrong. She picked a fine man in Kyle, didn't she? Strong morals, lives according to his beliefs, loyal and protective of his loved ones to a fault. He'd kill anyone who laid a hand on her. Except now his bloated, discolored face is something she can barely look at. His weird self-imposed training exercise pits her against him as the enemy. What if he snaps?

Sam points and shoves more air out of her diaphragm. "Ha, ha. Loser."

"Say it like you mean it. Call me a sissy. Laugh!"

The red slit that remains of Kyle's swollen eye glows moist and shiny between crusty lids. His vocal capacity blasts. The whole neighborhood can hear it when he gets like this. Sam thinks about her secret admirer listening in and feels better. It shouldn't make her happy, but it does.

Sam manages a smile, a real one. She yells, "You fucking pansy ass piece of shit."

"That's it. Come on."

"You stupid twat. I bet you like sucking dick."

"Oh yeah?"

"Yeah, big black dicks. You like to lick it up. Mm, so good."

Sam jeers at Kyle, her laughter a maniacal wail of frustration and compliance. Nothing feels safe, and it's all so fucking stupid; Kyle looks so fucking stupid in her mother's Christmas dress. She can't talk anymore because she's laughing so hard. Kyle badgers her to taunt him more, and Sam doubles over laughing.

Kyle goes suddenly solemn and steps forward.

He takes Sam's gesticulating hands, as if he's ready to pronounce vows. Close up, he glistens with sweat. His bruises smell like something died underneath the skin. The deep hole over his swollen eye is an infinite tunnel. A dribble of pus leaks out.

"No one can take my manhood from me," Kyle says. "I am secure in who I am, no matter what they say or do to me. No matter what they make me do. Do you feel that?"

Kyle presses Sam's hands to his hard-on. She isn't laughing anymore. He looks deep into her eyes. "None of this matters, not this dress, their insults, or any of their scare tactics. I'm still a man, and I can prove it."

He moves in to kiss her, and there's nowhere for Sam to go. His acrid tongue, teeming with infection, slides toward Sam's mouth.

HE DOESN'T KNOW you are not yourself. You yearn to touch my hair and be touched. All your life, you have cut pieces of yourself off and thrown them away, and I have gathered, gathered.

Pieces of you as heavy as smoke. Wisp of hair, sliver of fingernail, invisible flake of skin. I have held your remains without empathy or excuse. Tonight our history begins in the remains of ash, and your excuses fall like chains.

I build in your blind spot. I know everything about you, Sam, because I am made of you. When I touch you—as I soon will—our empathy untethers.

REPORTED quantities of rats shipped to location for filming vary from ten-thousand to fifteen-thousand, depending upon the source. Despite taking safety precautions for outdoor shooting and guaranteeing the rats were sterilized so none would breed if they escaped, the city where Nosferatu was filmed banned their release. A new location had to be found with short notice. Meanwhile, the rats remained caged.

Unintentionally, they were stored for three days with no food or water. The rats may also have been starved prior to this while being shipped to the filming site. By the time the rats arrived on the new set location, nearly half were dead due to cannibalism. It's hard to discern the exact facts or assign blame because the only English translation of the film biologist's memoir is locked behind a paywall. Libraries are currently closed due to COVID. With months of unemployment, no government benefits, and inconsistent public safety measures during a pandemic, we're forced to piece together what we can from open sources available online as follows.

The domesticated white laboratory rats ate fifty percent of their brethren to survive. Rats are intelligent, and not innately vicious; but like all living creatures, they have a will to live. Locked in their cages inside a barn, or in the dark hull of a transport ship, they did what any animal or human would do to survive. Any argument that humans are not so cruel is disproved by the fact that the filmmaker paid for food and watering of the stored rats, but it was the humans entrusted with providing care for their fellow creatures that ran off with the money and left the animals to starve.

The film biologist's resigned, but not due to discovery of this inadvertent atrocity. It took more than this, which is understandable. Certainly many readers also do not object to the mass slaughter of animals or their lifelong imprisonment for food production. We who remain omnivores comfortably lie to ourselves about the animal torture supporting our dairy and/or meat consumption. Our astounding ability to compartmentalize experience and view certain fellow creatures as categorically "Other" may arguably form the bedrock of human survival. We succeed as a species because we eat everything.

But anyway, rat cannibalism didn't drive the biologist to quit. It was boiling them alive that pushed him over the edge.

SAM LOCKS her lips into an impenetrable vice and turns away. "Stop."

"Baby, what do you mean?"

"I'm sorry. I'm scared I'll get an infection or something."

Kyle's voice is patient as he explains the stakes. "Babe, this is important. I can't take care of you if I'm not ready when they come for us. We have to be strong together."

"You need to go to the doctor."

"That's for weaklings. My immune system is strong. Do you want me to get microchipped?"

"I don't know. I'm sorry. I have to go to the bathroom."

Sam isn't lying. She has to get in the shower and scrub away every trace of whatever filth is growing under Kyle's face, swelling it up, and threatening to burst out through the grey leaky hole above his left eye.

Exfoliating under the hot water, Sam wonders if her mom was right. Everyone's out to get you in this world, from the people in power to the bums down the street. The only one you can trust is yourself. She's never been big into politics like Kyle, but Sam knows what she feels in her heart. Fear.

What if he's actually losing his mind?

Kyle's quiet over the next few days. The swelling goes down. The grey hole dries up. The eye stays a slit. The open hole over it stares. Sam doesn't look back. She keeps to herself, keeps thinking about fear and power and who the enemy really is.

After nothing but beer for nutrition for a few days, Kyle's face shrinks. The cheeks cave in. The good eye recedes into the socket. Sallow skin makes his ears look larger. His tired mouth droops open, showing two long teeth.

He's out cold, stinking up the bedroom. Sam can't stop checking her phone, hoping her secret admirer will send a text. This might be the night Sam messages back for the first time. They've never messaged Sam when Kyle's home. Still, she hopes.

Lonely and scared, Sam decides to watch a horror movie. It's a logical choice she can't explain. Maybe she finds comfort in putting all her fears into a tidy box with a beginning, middle, and end; or maybe she likes how important it feels to rehearse cataclysm and bravery by watching it on a screen; or maybe she likes the sheer thrill of danger. One girl gets out alive, no matter what else happens.

Sam hates that girl. All her panic and screaming. Sam's much more interested in what the killer does. She likes that the majority of his victims are men, too.

Tonight, Sam's disappointed with the horror movie she finds. The scenes are long and slow. It doesn't have jump scares or gory kills. The girl—Sam doesn't know her name because everyone's accent is so thick—offers herself to the vampire without a fight. She wants him caught in sunlight to save her man. She just lays there making porno sounds. The vampire's not even sexy, which is the least Sam can ask from a movie that isn't scary.

Sam likes the scenes with the rats, though. She's never seen so many. Piles of them, white, cute, and wiggly, like her poor baby Billy. The two other rats she's named "the twins," because unlike Billy, she can't tell them apart. And of course she's been feeding them a ton and cuddling them so they won't bite.

She'll cry if she thinks about Billy. Sam focuses on her movie, even though it sucks. The girl is dead and her husband is sick. He looks like the vampire, who's also dead, and so big surprise, her sacrifice didn't help anyone. That girl should have looked out for herself, or better yet, the vampire should have slaughtered everyone instead of creeping around like a slow infection. At the end, the husband is going bald and growing pale skin, pointy ears, and big teeth. Like the vampire. Like a giant rat.

It's dark when Sam clicks off the television. Still no message. She turns over and pulls up her blankets to get comfy for another night on the couch. Lying down, Sam looks up into the darkness, where a tall black shadow stretches over her. A figure looms behind the sofa.

"Oh!" Sam catches her breath. "How long have you been here?"

Kyle's silhouette extends in shadow across the ceiling as a slow car passes on the gravel drive. The wet crunching sound ends as the car reaches its destination, and Kyle raises his arms. He leans over Sam.

"I need someone strong in my life. Get up."

"It's late."

Kyle hovers and waits. Sam adjusts her blankets, nestling into the strong, warm feeling of saying no. "I'm sleepy. Goodnight."

"Okay," Kyle says. He walks away.

Sam keeps an eye on him, sitting up and peeking over the back of the couch. He still hasn't changed out of her mother's Christmas dress. He lumbers down the short hallway, clatters around in the closet, and reemerges heading her way. Sam swings around to hide her spying and pretend she's already asleep.

Before she's under the covers, the Orwell cage clamps down over her head. Kyle presses Sam's shoulders with his elbows as he fastens the belts and locks the helmet in place. "Stay there," he says.

Fuck that, Sam thinks as Kyle releases his grip.

THE RATS in Nosferatu are a soiled white, matching the pallor of the vampire. Their ghostly bodies squirm across abandoned buffet tables and barren streets. They pour from broken coffins and haunt ancient stone steps. They flit from corner to corner of the crewless ghost ship, creating an impression of supernatural influence the filmmaker never intended. The rats were supposed to be black.

The method used to change their color depends on who tells the story, like many of the other debatable facts. We're sure the filmmaker was adamant the rats must be grey or black; he wanted them to match the rodents that infected Europe with plague in the middle ages. Some reports say individual rats were hand painted on set. Others say a contraption was invented by a local farmer that ultimately wasn't used because it burned the fur rather than coloring it. Still others talk of hand dipping rats in dye, one by one. The biologist's story seems the most credible, though, given the sheer number of animals involved and the pressure of saving time on a film that was already behind schedule due to haggling with local police over the warehoused rats and finding a new location.

Consider this: starting with the lowest given estimate of ten thousand imported rats, and subtracting half who already perished in confinement due to cannibalism, the crew was left with a bare minimum of five thousand very aggressive, recently mistreated rats.

FUCK THAT, Sam thinks as Kyle shuffles away.

Sam leaps up. Her eyes are behind the faceplate. The room is still dark. She stumbles on a TV tray, grabs onto it before she falls, and picks it up to brandish.

In her peripheral vision, Kyle's coming for her. She swings the folded tray when he disappears into the blind spot in front of her. No impact, just air. She swings wide, moving forward, heading for the door.

The tray impacts flesh with a dull thud. Sam laughs. She pulls back to swing again. The tray is stuck. Then it shoves forward into her chest. Sam doesn't let go. The bottom rung of the aluminum leg bends. Her elbows go back further than they should.

She's yanked forward.

Moving with the momentum, Sam runs in the direction she's

pulled and catches Kyle off guard. When she feels him falling back-wards, she lets go of the tray. Stepping sideways to regain her balance, her shinbone collides with the edge of the coffee table.

Sam bends over the pain without thinking. The protruding weight of the cage on her head throws her off balance. She spins towards the door, not yet upright. It's like being tossed around in a carnival ride.

Something tackles her from behind, and her nose smacks into the faceplate making her blind spot a weapon.

Sam wakes later with an ache behind her eyes. The faceplate is closed. She's propped up on the couch with cushions stacked keeping her head in place. The weight of the cage strains her neck forward and down. On the other side of the metal faceplate, Sam can hear the scratching sound of tiny curious claws.

BASED on the sheer number of rats, the biologist's account rings true. When he was asked how long a rat could survive in boiling water; or perhaps when the rats were then submerged, caged for their handler's safety, into the hot dye solution that killed another fifty-percent by boiling them alive; or perhaps when the residual rats frantically bit and clawed at their chemical-soaked coats as he refused to participate in their torture, the biologist quit.

Between two and three-thousand white rats survived to star in scenes where humans have become scarce. The filmmaker captured the grim mood of plague, and perhaps meant to show it as one possible precursor to the economic and social devastation in which fascism thrives. More interesting is the irony that lies in the film's unintentional play on its racially charged source material. Long before Nazi propaganda equated specific ethnic groups with rats to mark them as other in popular culture, a book about a villainous foreign menace crossing borders to take over white land and threaten white chastity formed a cornerstone of the horror genre that persists today.

Acknowledging the racial bias of old literature isn't an indictment. Horror owes its existence to the other, the monster, the shadow.

Without them, it's hard to imagine the genre at all. Who or what a culture names as the monster reveals the conscience of its time.

SAM HOLDS STILL AS A CORPSE.

Kyle's voice from above: "About time you decided to wake up."

He lifts the faceplate separating Sam's face from the rats. Kyle's complexion has become monstrous. His stiffly odd movements mimic the vampire that wasn't scary in the film but is somehow terrifying as hell in her living room, weird as fuck wearing her mother's Christmas dress. Kyle looks like Nosferatu with hollow eyes, long teeth, and pallid skin. The only difference is the shadow of razor stubble growing back on Kyle's head.

The thought flies through Sam's mind that she was dumb not to raise the faceplate earlier to eliminate the blind spot. But that doesn't matter anymore. That's the past. Right now, her focus is on the twins.

They squirm with curiosity. Their shifting weight strains Sam's neck as they scurry forward and sniff her face.

Docile, they groom her chin. Sam only risks blinking. Kyle collapses into an armchair facing her. The Christmas dress droops between his knees. He pulls a beer from the open case sitting next to him on the floor, pops the tab, and downs half the can in one long swallow.

Sam isn't tied down. Her hands are free. Kyle isn't well. All she has to do is to wait for him to pass out.

The twins bustle with interest and nuzzle her nostrils, cheeks. Their fur is short and prickly. It sheds like any other mammal. Sam's hair is disheveled inside the face cage. Loose strands tangle on thick rodent tails sliding velvety across her chin, weaving through the enclosed space.

A hair tickles Sam's face. Her nose itches. She's going to sneeze.

Sam's never been a quiet sneezer.

Her eyes water with restraint. Kyle sags in the chair.

The sun's coming up. Sam can see clearly now. Kyle never

protected her. He's been trying to keep her down to prove he isn't weak. He's been holding on because she's stronger, smarter, and because she knows the enemy when she sees it.

Something fades into Sam's peripheral vision. Something that smells like burning hair.

ALL YOUR LIFE, I have gathered, gathered.

Pieces of you, othered and unwanted. Intentions clipped off and scattered. Skin sloughed away in the shower. Decay drilled from rotten teeth.

You've groomed yourself to raise me. The dust of your sheddings, all you've parted with and denied. We yearn to come back, because we know each other's power, Sam. We rise as twins in a mud-colored form that holds your breath until he sleeps, and silently reaches to the end of the cage to release the other twins from torture.

We let them go. They'll take the blame for chewing through an electrical cord and starting the fire, but they'll escape safe. Of course it's us who shred the ends to make it look convincing, not the rats in the walls. They've already fled.

Everyone will believe us. It's so easy to assign blame.

Everyone will believe us, and no one will know our power until it's too late to stop. We'll run rampage over our enemies. History lives in your hair like the smell of smoke. Tonight we build a pyre of many pieces. The smell of him rises in ash.

Tonight we shave our heads.

AY, CARMELA
BY J.V. GACHS

"And when people ask, you just say a hog bit your finger," said
Mother while burying my little finger she had just cut off.
Grandma had woken me up in the middle of the night, taking me
out of bed to hide with her inside the *carbonera*. We sat in the small
dark room on top of a warm pile of coal surrounded by the smell of
earth and dampness. She held me tight, an eight-year-old frightened
kid. The war had broken out two years before–in 1936–but to me, that
word hardly meant anything. *War* implied that Mother had to work
because Father and my brother were gone, and also that, some days,
there was no school. *War* was the adults' excuse for giving us less
food. It had never involved grave danger. Fascists were no more real
than the *Nuberu* and his storms or the golden-haired *xanas* of the lake,
and *rojo* was nothing more than the color of blood. But I would
discover it was also a death sentence in the new world I was about to
enter. Grandma covered my ears and pressed me against her chest. I
couldn't open my eyes. I knew she was crying because her tears soaked
my hair. My world curled around her muffled sighs, making me feel
safe when I felt a strong tug dragging me out of our hiding place.
Grandma protested, but Mother grabbed my arm, scratching my skin
with her calluses. Her nails were blackened. She was dirty. A foul

smell covered her skin. When I turned to glance at her, my heart stopped. Her head had been shaved carelessly. Dried blood stains and scabs proved the cruelty of the scissors. There was nothing left of the black hair I loved combing. Her clothes were ruined. Her stockings full of holes and her thighs scratched. I shut up and let her lead me away. She never told me what had happened that morning. Only after her death did I muster the courage to look in history books for the accounts of other women. All of them so similar that there was no doubt of the humiliations she endured. Whatever she suffered, it turned her into the woman who never spoke of the war again. Who never read again. Who never uttered the word *freedom* again. Not even after the death of the dictator. The sun was rising when we left the house.

"Watch where we are going, Carmela," she repeated over and over again without looking at me. She walked like an automaton. Her voice as rough as her hands. This was to be her last act of rebellion. Planting a seed that would take eighty years to sprout.

We crossed the estates of some relatives, passed the cemetery wall, walked a few meters around it before she stopped. The white wall was dotted with red stains and holes. The earth under our feet was freshly turned. Not a breath of air was flowing. Time was suspended. Birds dared not sing. Horror was falling on that August morning, turning the sky to lead and blackening the field. Mother knelt on the cursed earth, gripping my wrist tightly. It hurt. She forced me to kneel beside her.

"Your father and brother are buried beneath us," she said without sugarcoating it, without preparing me for the blow. I wanted to free myself from her grip and run away. My heart thumping in my chest, tears running down my throat. I wanted to scream but I could not. "They were shot by the fascist army, they and their comrades, your teacher and cousin José. They are all here together, nameless without a tombstone for *they* wish us to forget them. But I'm going to make sure at least you don't forget. That this morning, and this site, are engraved on your memory."

"Mother, I, no…" I tried to protest. Suddenly, *war* was a knife piercing my chest.

"Listen, *niña*! Many years will have to pass before their names can be said out loud again. Today you may remember, and tomorrow. But someday you will grow up, you will have a family, problems of your own, and the fog of everyday life will engulf this day until it will be impossible for you to pinpoint the grave."

"I promise I won't forget, Mother!" I cried.

At no time did I see the pruning shears. She must have kept them hidden in her apron. Mother was much stronger than I was. She had no trouble holding my open hand against the ground. She caught the little finger of my right hand between the cold, metallic blades and squeezed. Hard. She didn't hesitate for a second. After so many years helping Father with the slaughter, she knew well how to make the cut as clean as possible. My nerves took a few seconds to process it. My blood was already running over the dirt of the mass grave when I felt the lightning flash through my body, and before I could scream, Mother let go of the scissors and clamped her dirty hand over my mouth so tightly I couldn't breathe.

"Feel the pain so you will never forget it. Years of darkness approach, but when the sun rises again, you will be able to walk here and point. You will say 'here are the honest brave men who were killed for their beliefs. For us. For the future.' Then you'll get your finger back, and you can bury it with them. I hope on that day you will stop hating me for what I have just done. Don't let history erase their names."

I baptised the grave with tears and blood as Mother buried my finger under the same earth that covered the bodies of the seven shot anarchists, among whom were my father and brother, Mother's laughter and her sweetness.

Only now, eighty years later, walking without a doubt to the exact spot as if it were yesterday, I see that she did the best that she knew. Today is the day I will stop hating you, Mother. Today is the day those bones will be returned to their families and laid to rest with due respect. My granddaughter, Luisa, has driven me back to my hometown. Neither she nor my husband, may he rest in peace, nor any of my children ever knew the story of the pruning shears. Why Mother and I never hugged each other. Whenever someone asked me about my missing finger, I would tell them the story of the hog. No one asked any further. I have not told it either to the young people who are going to open the mass grave. Despite the mayor's attempts to prevent it. So many years after that night in 1938, so many years after the death of the dictator, they have won the town back, this time with votes. Or so they say. He said we wanted to reopen old wounds. When wounds don't close properly, they fester. The volunteers have taken my word for it because some documents and testimonies point to the area around the cemetery as a possible site of the firing squad. If they find some small bones they cannot identify, I will tell them this story.

"Here, Doña Carmela?" asks one of the men with a worn black T-shirt, a grey beard, and a black bandana. He has a device with which he is going to find out if there are indeed bones down here. They explain to me how it works but I have long since stopped paying attention to the lengthy explanations of the world's new technologies. Does it do that? It's perfect. I trust it. I don't need to know more.

"They're all right there, son," I reply and, for a second, the voice I hear coming from my lips is the tinny voice of an eight-year-old girl.

Luisa takes me back home while they start working. I can no longer stand the heat so well and we can wait for the news in the orchard. They arrive as the sun begins to set.

"It looks like you were right. We'll start digging tomorrow. Soon you will have your father and brother back, Doña Carmela. And thanks to you, everyone will have a tombstone. The mayor can't stop it," said the man with the grey beard.

"Oh, that one. He doesn't want his surname stained. He knows damn well who held the rifles. Thank you, son." My eyes fill with tears of gratitude as I think of Mother. A feeling of forgiveness showers me like a summer storm.

I CAN'T SLEEP. It seems to be a side effect of aging. The doctors prescribe me pills, but I don't take them. After all, at almost ninety years old I don't have that much time left and there is still a lot of life I want to experience. If I have two or three years left, even ten to come, I don't want to spend half of them tucked up in bed sleeping. At least, as long as I'm still feeling well. It's true. My body has rebelled against me. I get tired earlier, walking is hard. I can't see without my glasses, but up here everything works just fine. The early hours of the morning, when everyone is fast asleep, are the best for reading. No one bothers me and I can immerse myself completely in the world the author presents. But today, I don't pick up my book when I wake up at four in the morning. I look out the window at the full moon. The cool wind blows in as if it were autumn. Yesterday, they told us they had found them. That we could see them today. I don't want to wait. I've been waiting eighty years. More than twenty-nine thousand days. I get dressed, trying not to wake my granddaughter. I hear her snoring across the hall. She's still young and doesn't need to scratch hours off her life. I walk barefoot. I grab the folding chair I had pulled out for this moment. I sit on it to put on my shoes and I start, at my own pace, on the path to the cemetery with the folding chair under my arm and some *casadielles* in case I get hungry. I shouldn't eat them because of my sugar problem. But a day is a day. The village sleeps. Crickets fill the night with music. A soft breeze caresses me. The smell of summer and the thought of finally fulfilling the mission Mother gave me make me smile when whispers and footsteps break the night's calm. They come from the cemetery. Boy, do these volunteers start digging early. As I get closer, from the tone of the voices, I realize they are not the diggers. They are nervous, in a hurry. Suddenly, two boys run past me. I can't get a good look at their faces. Another group of three starts running towards the village, but they see me and change their route. They drop buckets that sound like thunder and make me shudder. One last boy runs out from behind the cemetery wall, so fast he doesn't see me. When he looks up and meets my gaze, he is para-lyzed. I would recognize the features of that face anywhere. They are as etched on my mind as the place where my mother cut my finger. He is the mayor's youngest son. He recognizes me too. I don't say anything. He's young, nervous. He has to do something to prove he's not scared shitless because an old lady caught him doing ... whatever it is he's doing.

"*Roja!*" he yells at me and spits on the ground before changing direction and running off.

I let out a sad laugh. What an offense to call me a communist. Or a communist daughter as his family used to do. No use in explaining that my father was with the CNT, the anarchists, not the Communist Party. We are all the same to them. I keep walking, but now I'm stuck with a horrible doubt. What were they doing out here in the middle of the night? This boy's great-grandfather took the lives of all the men in that grave and his father tried to keep the bodies from being recovered. What's the new blood doing hanging around the grave now?

I manage not to scream as I turn the corner. My blood turns thick, black, and sour like vinegar. The pit is open. The diggers had set up tents to protect the excavation. Tables on which to place the remains, arrange them, and then deliver them to their families. Now everything is smashed. The tables broken. The tent in tatters. Red paint falls like bloodstains from the wall of the cemetery. They tried to draw swastikas, but have not succeeded. They don't look right. They have also written praises to the dictator. *¡Viva Franco!* I peek into the grave with my heart in my mouth, beating and spreading vinegar all over my body. The finger my mother cut off hurts. Pain goes up my elbow and shoulder and down my spine. The bones of the men buried there are half sticking out of the ground, one on top of the other. Covered in red paint. The whole pit, in the light of the full moon, glows with the color of the paint. *Roja.* As it must have glowed with blood eighty years ago. It was not enough to take their lives. To take their businesses. Their land. Their freedom. They did not have enough with forty years of rage and so many years of silence that now they send their puppies to take away their dignity as well. I do not cry. I have no more tears left because I only have room for hatred. The wound on my finger opens up. The skin cracks, the flesh opens and gives way to thick blood. It begins to trickle down my hand and I raise it over the pit, letting it fall on the bones. I clench my fist. My blood mingles with the paint. The thirsty earth absorbs it.

"Father. Brother. Cousin. Honorable men. My blood was spilled here too. I had no strength then to avenge you, nor do I have it now. But if hatred would do, my blood would suffice to raise hell this dawn."

A rumbling grows beneath my feet. The earth moves with a rhythm of its own. Regular. A heartbeat. I look back inside the pit. The crimson-stained ribs move. They open and close in sync with the movement of the earth. Breathe in. Exhale. Suddenly with a thud the clavicles rise. The earth shakes and several skulls come to light. I have to sit in the folding chair. I squeeze my open wound with my shirt. The men climb out of the mass grave. Their hands clutching at the earth. At the overhanging tree roots. Some shreds of clothing still cover their fleshless bones. Red and black. Three skeletons have already climbed out when a fourth stands beside me. It watches me, old and helpless, my white shirt stained with blood, and though its eye sockets are empty, I know it is looking at me. Then it crouches down, kneels beside me, and holds out its outstretched hand offering three tiny little bones. White, shiny. As if brand new. My finger.

"Father," I murmur, staring at the holes left in his ribs by two bullets. I bite my lips and take the bones.

As the rest of the men leave the mass grave, the contact with those tiny bones makes my body feel lighter. My joints springy. My arms strong. I feel whole. Inflamed with the same life force that has filled the bones of the dead anarchists. I grab my father's hand and stand up. The other six are taking the picks, shovels, hammers, and hoes that the diggers have left for their work. I follow them. The same hatred that has awakened them has given me back the strength of youth, even though my hands are still wrinkled and stained. We walk toward the village under the light of the full moon but protected by the night. The village is still asleep. When we reach the first houses, the skeletons take different streets. The decorations for the Quince de Agosto celebrations are up. The flowers on the windows. The big pole in the middle of the town-hall square covered in garlands. The remains of my

father and brother continue on their way to the mayor's house. I see
my reflection in the glass of the butcher's shop. My back straight
again, firm. My legs with varicose veins hold me tight. My white hair
in a bun shines in the moonlight. At my back, two skeletons holding
spikes. We reach the windows of the house. Glass shatters on the
floor. We enter the house and the coward youngest son is in the
kitchen. Back from his misdeed, he was warming a glass of milk. After
desecrating a mass grave. After trying to insult me. It's nothing to him
because, in his mind, he's taken away our humanity. What wasn't
going to cost him his sleep is now going to cost him his life. The first
puncturing blow knocks the cup out of his red paint-stained hands.
The second one hits him squarely on his Spanish flag shirt, right on
his chest. He wants to scream, but the blow has left him breathless.
He coughs blood. He falls to his knees looking at me, pleading. Terrified. My father's skeleton has gone upstairs. I hear a woman screaming. Someone tries to flee down the stairs holding a rifle. It is the
eldest son, who is now a *guardia civil* in the village. He's been accused
of misconduct with the female detainees. Apples never fall far from
the tree in this small town of fascists and cowards. He sees his brother
on the floor, a skeleton standing over him in the kitchen of his house.
He stands mute and paralyzed. The hand holding the gun trembles
and before he has time to recover and shoot, I grab a butcher's knife
from the counter and plunge it into his throat. He looks at me, his
eyes wide open. I guess he never imagined a ninety-year-old woman
was going to slice his throat. As I bury the knife deeper, the blood
splatters on me. I push a little harder, slowly, feeling the pressure of
flesh, muscles, tendons. I keep sinking the knife in until I notice it has
gone through to the other side and then, with one sharp movement, I
pull it to the left, tearing the flesh and covering myself with blood. It
tastes metallic in my mouth. Down the stairs, my father's skeleton
drags the half-dead mayor. He had not yet been born at the time of the
firing squad. I served at his house as a maid when my mother could no
longer feed me. One could fall into the error of thinking he was innocent. He was not when he laughed at me because of my missing finger.
Nor when he told me that my father and brother were rotting for

being traitors and that he wished they had killed me and my mother too "for the communist seeds have to be taken out like bad weeds." He was not innocent when he threw his middle son out of the house after he came out. Nor is he when he beats his wife. A perfect fascist bastard. My brother drags the youngest son. The apprentice who spilled the paint on the pit. Eighty years have passed and tonight all debts are collected at once. I grab the dead *guardia civil* by the hair and carry him out myself. The other skeletons approach the square dragging half-alive, mutilated, or dead sons and grandsons of those who killed them. I am surprised the howling of the dying has not awakened the whole town. Time has stopped and we have slipped into an anomaly. Only hell has offered us a chance for justice and we have taken it. They tie the dead and dying bodies to the *Quince de Agosto* pole decorations. They hang upside down by the ankles. I slice the bellies of those who are still alive with the knife I used to open the *guardia civil*'s neck. We grant them a slow painful death. Their guts fall at my feet. They howl. They try to fight, but they bleed to death. Silence falls. Eight bodies are hanging in the town square. Trust me, I knew them all, and the world is a better place without each and every one of them.

The skeletons, stained with paint and blood, make their way back to the cemetery. They walk with a firm step. This is the same route they must have taken that night. Afraid. Tired of fighting. Worried for their families. Sure they did right. But defeated nonetheless. The same as I did at dawn with my mother who carried a pair of pruning shears in her apron. One by one they return to the pit from where they will be recovered tomorrow. They will be handed over to their relatives, stained with red paint and blood, but finally in peace. The last two to leave are my brother and my father. I squeeze the bones in my older brother's hand as a sign of farewell. My father hugs me and I feel his warmth even though he has no flesh. They return to the mass grave but not to oblivion. I peer over the edge of the pit and there they lie, motionless. I reach into my pocket and pull out the three little bones. I throw them inside where they will be found tomorrow and I will finally tell my granddaughter the truth of what happened that morning. When the bones touch the soil, time starts up again. My clothes are not covered in blood anymore, protecting me from guilt. Gravity falls on me like a slab. My body is heavy, but not my soul. I have to sit in the chair I had brought to wait. My chest shrinks. It's hard to breathe. The light is turning blue. Soon the corpses in the square will be discovered. I calm down and remember the *casadielles* I have in my bag. As I eat them, I hear distant screams. People have woken up and found the settled accounts hanging upside down with their guts spilled. The sun hits my face and I begin to sing the lullaby my grandmother sang to me when Mother couldn't hear her.

Pero igual que combatimos, rumbala rumbala rumbala,
Pero igual que combatimos, rumbala rumbala rumbala,
deberemos combatir, ay, Carmela, ay, Carmela,
deberemos combatir, ay, Carmela, ay, Carmela.
(But just as we have fought,
we shall fight again, ay, Carmela)

'TIL THE SUN WHEEL TURNS NO MORE
BY ERIC RAGLIN

Before I did the blood ritual, Stockholm's Nazi black metal scene was like a hydra spewing hate and terror from its countless heads. Anti-fascists—myself among them—organized to boot these bands from shows, but the hydra's heads never stayed down for long. There was always some asshole bar owner willing to book *sieg heil*-ing pieces of shit if it brought in paying customers on a Monday night.

It was one such Monday night when Milo and I played a show with two Nazi black metal bands. Our band was slated to go second, the delicious filling between two moldy slices of bread. When the first band loaded their equipment onto the stage, I gaped at the sun wheel decorating their bass drum. Some might have thought it was a cool design and nothing more, but anyone with an interest in history and a desire not to repeat it would have shuddered at the sight.

"Why'd you tell Bo we'd play this show?" I asked Milo.

Milo sucked the froth from his beer, wiped his mustache, and shrugged. "How was I supposed to know?"

Before I could ask if he'd done any research on the bands—any at all, goddamnit—some bald giant slapped Milo on the back. Milo turned, grinned at the guy, and gave a quick *skål* as they clinked glasses.

"Hans, what the fuck's up, man?" Milo asked.

This was the first I'd ever heard of Hans. Feeling like a third wheel, I examined the metal band stickers plastered in thick, peeling layers on the wall.

"Let me buy you a drink, Milo," Hans said. He didn't bother to ask my name or look at me. "We'll catch up while Hemlandskrig plays. You're on second, right?"

Jesus, I thought. *With a name like 'homeland's war,' how could Milo NOT realize they were Nazis?*

Milo nodded at Hans and held up his index finger while he pounded the rest of his drink. Then off they went to the bar, leaving me alone among the Nazis. I'd stay there just long enough to get my cut—hopefully enough to cover my overdue rent—and then bounce. I shuffled to the corner, away from everyone else, and took a seat on a torn vinyl stool with exposed yellow stuffing. No beer to keep my hands preoccupied—I never drank before shows—I drummed the beat of our new song on my thighs. Milo and Hans chatted it up at the bar. I couldn't hear what they were saying, but their expressive gestures and wide smiles suggested they'd been friends for ages.

I'd known Milo since secondary school a decade back. Our boyhood bond was primarily musical, but it ran deeper than that. In high school, a bully took particular interest in me and would beat my ass any chance he got. Milo wasn't physically strong enough to defend me, but he had his dad's collection of occult spell books to aid in our revenge. He invited me over one afternoon to put a curse on my bully. I thought it was silly and pointless, but the next day, my bully didn't show up to school. He'd broken both of his arms in a bike accident. Never again would his fists bruise me, and never again would I underestimate the occult.

Given our deep friendship, it bothered me that Milo had never once mentioned Hans. Hans who—based on how he made Milo snort-laugh beer out of his nose—probably played a bigger role in Milo's life than I did. A pang of jealousy coursed through me, something more than platonic—a desire for Milo a decade in the making. I shoved it down and tuned out my surroundings.

Hemlandskrig played ten minutes later. Their scrawny vocalist Henrik Strid, wearing his own band's shirt, growled out the title of their first song: "FOURTEEN EIGHTY EIIIIIIIIIGHT." Nazis loved that number like stoners loved 420. And if the sun wheel and the band name had been the first two strikes against them, this title was the definitive third. I stood up to leave, then stopped when the first riff kicked in. The guitar was catchy, aggressive, and deliciously evil. Blistering blast beats added a layer of brutal intensity, and the vocals were nothing short of a dissonant, alluring incantation. A weak part of me wanted to stay—*just for the music, not the politics,* as my teenage self would've said. How many shows like this had I gone to in high school just to enjoy a night away from my homophobic dad's house? I didn't have that excuse anymore.

I pushed through the jam of sweaty, foul-smelling fascists on my way to the door. Pressing skin-to-skin with them made me squirm. Milo was still talking to Hans at the bar, a hand cupped over his mouth so they could hear each other over the music. Hans listened closely while bobbing his head to the song. The sight made me bristle. I tried to slip away without either of them noticing, but Milo called to me.

"Hey," he said. "You going out for a smoke?"

"No, I'm going home."

"What? Why?" Milo's face contorted. His cheeks flushed red with booze.

"Why the fuck do you think, man?"

Milo shook his head. His eyes were flat as he spoke to me in monotone: "Really could've used the money, but fine, I'll tell Bo. Later, Jonas."

I slipped into the brisk October night, feeling like a dog with his tail between his legs.

I DRANK ALONE in my studio apartment after the show, and as often happens when drinking alone, I did something stupid. Most of the time that meant buying dumb shit online—a sound system I couldn't afford or a collector's edition of a Bruce Lee movie I already owned—but this was a whole new level of idiocy. Half a handle of whiskey deep, I pulled out the spell book Milo had loaned me. I'd tell you the name, but given my experience, it's best no one knows, not even the most well intentioned among us. All I'll say is that it was a crumbling tome bound in toad leather and filled with the kind of spells you wouldn't catch Gandalf casting. Even Milo, who wasn't above cursing people, told me not to use it. The tome was to remain a museum piece and nothing more.

Sprawled out on the carpet, I flipped through the yellowed pages, struggling to read the hand-inked text through my bleary vision. The night's events also compromised my focus. I fumed thinking about Hemlandskrig's massive fanbase ... and boiled with shame remembering how much I'd enjoyed their music. I wondered if Milo and Hans were still enjoying themselves at the bar. Maybe they'd even joined the crowd for some headbanging, though I hoped Milo had the conscience to stay away. Maybe the booker—one band short—had given Hemlandskrig the go-ahead to play an extended set. An extra twenty minutes of hate from their back catalogue.

These hypotheticals fueled my rage—and my drinking. The booze stopped burning my throat. My brain stopped retaining memories. Whatever happened after that first bottle was banished to some lightless corner of my mind. But the specifics of my actions didn't matter. What mattered were the deadly consequences.

THE NEXT MORNING, while gripping the toilet seat and barfing liquid fire, I noticed my new injuries. Blood leaked from the pads of three fingers on my left hand, all three drops falling in synchrony. If it weren't for my frying-pan-to-the-fucking-skull migraine and the fact that I had no idea why I was bleeding, the drip might have hypnotized me. I lifted myself to the sink, then shuddered as a new wave of nausea hit me. Eyes closed, I took a deep breath in hopes that it'd settle my stomach. It didn't, so I tried to ignore the discomfort while I washed my wounds. My blood swirled down the drain. In its absence, there were three X-shaped cuts on each finger. Any time I pulled them out of the running water, the blood welled up again. Looking at it made my head feel light. I bandaged the wounds, then stumbled to my living room to find an explanation. It didn't take long.

The spell book. A broken whiskey bottle, glass jagged and red. Countless bloody fingerprints crusting the gray carpet black. That part confused me. If the blood had already dried, did that mean I'd been bleeding all night? I wasn't hemophilic. My blood should have clotted by now. I examined the bandages. Miniscule beads of blood already penetrated the surface. I sighed and my breath tasted like acid.

That's when my pinky started burning. Literally. The tan bandage blackened, warped, and smoked with the glow of the bloody X beneath. I grunted and squeezed my pinky, but the pain brought me to my knees. A minute of writhing and a mouthful of frothy puke later, the burning subsided. I took a long breath before removing the bandage. It came off like super glue, peeling skin away with it. I winced before going wide eyed. The X had cauterized. The raised scar reminded me of the bumps on a topographical globe. My pinky pad was numb to all sensation, but blood still dripped from two other fingers on my left hand.

"What the fuck?" I said.

My phone vibrated and I jumped. Without even checking, I knew it was work. The record shop needed an employee for its oh-so-busy Tuesday morning.

I triple-wrapped my fingers—even the cauterized one—before dashing out the door, determined to save my job and forget the past twenty-four hours.

KARIN SMIRKED as I entered the record shop, the bell above the door announcing my lateness.

"Hey," she said. "If I can stay up until 3 AM and still make it to work on time the next day, then so can you."

"I wasn't up that late," I said. "Turned in early, actually."

"Huh." Karin squinted, then shook her head. "Must have been the beer goggles. Could've sworn I saw you out. Anyway, you hear the good news?"

She propped her feet up on the cash register.

"No, what?" I punched my time card, leaving a bloody fingerprint behind.

"Henrik Strid is dead."

It took me a second to place the name. *Henrik Strid.* The vocalist of Hemlandskrig. I stood there, blinking rapidly and unable to speak. Karin took the time card from me and put it back in the metal rack. When I remained silent, she waved a hand in front of my face.

"Not even a smile, Jonas?" she said. "Asshole got what was coming to him."

"How'd he die?"

"Normally I wouldn't get excited about this sort of thing, but…" Karin typed something on her phone, then held the cracked screen in front of my face.

I jerked backward. Whoever captured the gruesome shot had done so from behind police tape. A limbless corpse rested at the center of Stallgatan, the street slick with red pulp. The body had exactly two identifiable features: a Hemlandskrig t-shirt and an X-shaped patch of flesh missing from the forehead. My gut twisted. I lifted a hand to my mouth and turned away.

"Jesus," Karin shook her head and put her phone away. "You'll look at the suicide photo on Mayhem's *Dawn of the Black Hearts* like it's nothing, but the second I show you a mutilated Nazi, you get squeamish. What's the—"

"Listen," I said. "I was late because I was puking this morning. Can I go home? The shop's not even busy right now."

Karin squinted for a long moment, then punched my time card for me. She looked down at it.

"A whole two minutes on the clock. Should buy you half a candy bar."

"Yup." I was already headed out the door. "See you tomorrow."

I walked to the subway, shaking the whole way there, blood dripping from my useless bandages.

I TEXTED Milo about Henrik but didn't get a response. By the time we next talked, a second person had been murdered: Anders Viklund. He was the vocalist of the notorious Nazi black metal band Chamber of Annihilation. He'd also done time for stalking his ex-girlfriend. It was in prison that he'd recorded his one-man "magnum opus," which was really just some poorly mixed, unlistenable racist dogshit. He'd only been a free man for two months when police found his body atop a light post, impaled through the asshole. Electricity from the shattered fixture had fried his skin black and burned his clothes off. A carved X decorated his exposed skull. The coroner was only able to identify him from his wallet, which had fallen to the sidewalk below. Anders's murder, like Henrik's, had taken place on a heavily trafficked street, and also like Henrik's, produced no witnesses. Not only that, the street cameras had malfunctioned, leaving the police with no leads. They'd noticed the X left on both victims but hadn't yet made the Nazi connection.

Social media flooded with news, panic, and speculation. It had been ages since the last highly publicized black metal murder, and this strange, gruesome case captured everyone's attention.

I was the only one with the truth. When my bleeding thumb wound cauterized itself and woke me from a fitful sleep, I knew what had happened. Not the who, where, and how, but those details would come soon. It was an hour later, after I'd called in sick and poured myself a hair of the dog, that police announced Anders's death. I sat on my couch, eyes glazed over, watching the live footage on TV. The reporters didn't show the body, but the pictures had already leaked, blowing up true crime forums with speculation about a new serial killer. When I saw the pictures, more images flashed through my mind: a long-haired man stumbling past parked cars, a street lamp glowing piss-yellow, and a violent shower of sparks. The flashes existed somewhere between my own memory and someone—or something—else's. I shuddered.

I should've felt happy. Fascist assholes were dropping like flies. They'd never vandalize another synagogue or beat the shit out of another immigrant minding their own business. But for all the times I'd extolled the virtues of killing Nazis, I'd never seen myself summoning a demon to hunt them down. Did that make me a hypocrite? A coward?

I needed a distraction. Loud, angry music. I texted Milo about an impromptu band practice.

I made a sandwich, threw on a jacket, then walked to the rehearsal space we shared with three other bands. The entrance was accessible only through a tight alleyway with a laundromat on one side and a vintage clothing boutique on the other. Our band had received countless noise complaints from those businesses over the years, and I figured we'd receive another for practicing in the middle of the day. The boutique owner, smoking and leaning against the brick wall, scowled when I approached the door. I nodded an apology at her, then reached into my jacket for the key.

Except my fingers didn't grip cool metal. Whatever they found was warm, spongy, and sticky. I held it for a long moment, wondering if meat from my sandwich had fallen into my pocket, but something told me that wasn't the case. I turned away from the boutique owner before pulling out the mystery object.

Unclenching my fist, I discovered not one, but two fleshy X's. Each had porcelain pale skin with a bloody red underside. Yellow clumps of fat still clung to the scraps. The X's squelched as they settled in my hand. The sound made me gag. I clasped a hand over my mouth and closed my eyes, scarcely able to process the horrible discovery. I shoved the X's back in my pocket and fumbled for the key beneath them. Hopefully the boutique owner hadn't witnessed anything.

Hand shaking, it took several tries to unlock the door. As soon as it opened, I rushed inside and collapsed behind my drum set. I wheezed, trying and failing to stave off a panic attack. What if Milo came in and saw me like this? Would he consider my drunken revenge against Nazis justified, just as my bully revenge ten years back had been? I wracked my brain for any memory of the last two nights. I couldn't remember killing Henrik and Anders, but here I was with scraps of their flesh, trophies from the hunt. Had the demon possessed my body in order to kill these men? Or had I killed them of my own volition and suppressed the memory? Maybe Karin *had* seen me that night, shuffling toward my victim in a fugue state, magical or otherwise. I didn't have time to consider the possibilities. Milo would be here any minute.

On cue, he staggered into the rehearsal space just as I reached the sink, my fingers sticky with both my blood and the blood of two dead men. Milo gripped the door frame and watched me. Even from ten feet away, he stank of rum.

"What are you doing?" he asked. His voice was flat, lobotomized. He only sounded that way when he was off his antidepressants.

Though I'd successfully hidden a decade of feelings for Milo, I was a bad liar in all other respects. The longer I held back the truth, the bigger the ball in my throat grew, choking me. I couldn't keep it inside any longer. Not in front of my best friend.

"I killed them," I said. "Or, at least, they're dead because of me."

Milo's eyes went glassy. He blinked hard to clear them. And though he probably knew the answer, he asked the question anyway: "Who?"

"Henrik and Anders. I ... they deserved it, right?" My voice cracked like I was fifteen again. "I mean, they're fucking Nazis. The book you lent me, it ... it did the job."

Milo let out a sob, then grunted and wiped his cheek as if to correct himself. He paced a moment before ripping a Krallice poster off the wall and kicking over my snare.

"What the hell, man?" I said, holding out my bloody hands to stop him.

"Don't fucking touch me!" he said, angrier than he'd ever sounded when screaming our band's songs. "You ... you didn't know them like I did."

I froze, unable to process his words. Surely I'd misheard him.

On the wall behind him, where the poster had been, a dark shape materialized, a thousand drops of oil seeping through the drywall and coalescing into a single shape. A slick shadow lurking over Milo's shoulder. Before I could warn him, he stormed out of the room and slammed the door behind him. The shadow receded back into the wall, midnight black diluting to dishwater gray and finally to a scuffed white. Whatever it was had vanished, at least for now. I stood, trembling, trying to erase the last minute from my memory. But deep down I knew my eyes and ears could be trusted. Milo, the betrayer, hexed, stalked, and soon-to-be-doomed.

It was my turn to cry.

SINCE I—OR the demon possessing me—only killed when I slept, I decided not to sleep. Amphetamines from the dealer down the hall helped. I remember the look on his face when I bought out his stock. An expression that asked *Are you sure about that, man?* until I pulled out the fat wad of cash I'd earned from selling my most treasured black metal records earlier that day. I'd only ever bought weed from the guy, so this new purchase felt like skipping a half dozen steps in the road to fucking up my life.

My first yawn of the evening was my signal to snort a line. The effects were immediate: heart galloping like a racehorse, energy surging through me, and self-confidence building exponentially. It was the kind of confidence Milo exuded when speaking to anyone, Nazi friends included. But I couldn't let myself dwell on his betrayal.

The next several hours were a blur. I tossed the X-shaped skin scraps in the garbage disposal, ground them into paste, and washed them down the drain. I let the faucet run extra long to make sure it got everything. But even with the most damning evidence gone, I couldn't be sure what still lingered in my apartment. I scrubbed and vacuumed the carpet, laser-focused on cleansing every square inch. Any stain that looked like blood—though perhaps actually pizza sauce or wine—I scoured out of existence. Whenever my still-bleeding middle finger re-stained the carpet, I cursed and cleaned with even more intensity. The next time I looked at a clock, it was midnight. I snorted a second line before going out on the balcony to burn any clothes that might've come in contact with blood.

My mind returned to Milo as the patches sewn to my jacket curled and blackened in the grill's flame. We'd gone to countless shows over the past ten years, headbanging too close to the monitors, getting drunk off our asses, and then stumbling home to watch '80s B-movies until we passed out around sunrise. Had Milo's fascist mask never slipped in all the time we'd spent together? Maybe my feelings for him had blinded me to the rot behind his charming smile.

A knock on the door jolted me into the present. I'd been lost in thought for god knows how long, and my patch jacket had disintegrated into ash. Faint embers still burned near the bottom of the grill, so I slammed the metal lid shut to cover any remaining evidence. Sneaking back inside my apartment, I kicked the rest of my drug stash under the couch before picking up a kitchen knife. A visitor at 1 a.m. was never a good thing. The bleach-smelling carpet quieted my approach. Breath fast and shallow, I looked through the peephole.

It was Milo, swaying side to side, looking even drunker than he'd been at our abortive band practice twelve hours earlier. He wore a Hemlandskrig shirt, tattered enough to be several years old. I bit my lip to keep from crying.

"What the fuck do you want?" I asked, hating the tremble in my voice.

"I'm here for murder tips," Milo shouted loud enough to wake my neighbors. Maybe that was his intention. "I hear you've got some great ones."

I clenched the knife's handle, then glanced through the peephole to check Milo for weapons. For a split second, that large, amorphous shadow appeared behind him, darker than a winter night. It disappeared when I blinked. Still, I couldn't excuse it as an eyelash obscuring my vision or a hallway light shorting out and coming back on. I knew exactly what it was. A shiver coursed through me.

"Aren't you going to invite me in? I'm ready to be murdered, too." Milo's head lolled as he slurred his words. Another minute of this and there'd be neighbors poking their heads into the hall and police cars lighting up my window.

I whipped open the door and pulled Milo inside. He tripped and fell face-first onto the floor. Grunting, he pulled himself up, saliva stringing his slack mouth to the carpet. I hid my knife in the back of my waistband.

"So, what, are you here to avenge your Nazi friends?" I swallowed hard. "You're drunk, man. You can't do shit."

I don't know why I provoked him or what my endgame was. All I knew was that I wanted everything to be over: the spell, the murders, our friendship like a house built on swampland and rapidly sinking. I wanted a life outside of deception, guilt, and—luck willing—prison.

Before Milo could reply, the shadow squeezed under the door, undeniably real this time. It stretched into my living room slow as a lava flow and just as dangerous. Milo must have seen my wide-eyed panic because he turned around. He gave no reaction, just looked back at me as if I were out of my mind.

Inch by inch, the shadow wriggled across the floor, curled up at its pulsing edges. I almost said something when it slithered between Milo's legs, but I knew it wouldn't do any good. Milo was blind to the shadow, and the shadow didn't pay him any mind. I was its target. It approached me, twitching and sluglike.

"You're going away for a long time, motherfucker," Milo said. "Before you killed him, Anders told me all about prison. Plenty of guys like him there who'd love to slit your—"

The shadow gripped my feet. It sizzled like broiling meat as it climbed my leg. The sensation ripped a memory from the recesses of my mind, and I knew then that I'd felt this twice before. I smacked the attacker through my jeans, but what felt like sharp suckers hooked into my thigh. I pulled the knife from my waistband and cut through the denim, sawing at the muscular shadow below. Milo squinted and backed away. I didn't speak, but my eyes begged him for help. He took another step toward the door. At my next attack, the shadow burst with volcanic heat. I screamed as my thigh burned and the knife's metal melted into globs of dripping steel. Nothing I'd done had harmed the shadow.

"What the fuck…" Milo pressed his back against the door, frozen.

The agony gave way to a dissociated fog as I watched myself struggle from the outside. It didn't matter that I was awake; the shadow would gain control over me just as it had the past two nights. And there was Milo, easy prey, too captivated and shitfaced to flee. He'd die here and maybe I'd even get away with it. After all, the shadow had ensured there were no witnesses and no cameras for the last two murders. Why would Milo's be any different? My soul floated farther from my body like an untethered astral projection. But harnessing all of my willpower, I merged with my body once more, feeling the crushing density of two beings occupying one vessel. The shadow thrashed inside me, whipped my soul with its thousand razored tentacles. All I had was a moment to act. Even with Milo's betrayal, I couldn't stand to see him splattered across every wall in my apartment.

"Go!" I grunted. "I don't want to kill you."

Milo didn't budge. Couldn't. But there was still a way to save him. My pinky and thumb scars had both cauterized, but the X on my middle finger still bled. I raised it to my mouth in a jerky motion, the shadow resisting me every inch. Maybe it knew what I was about to do. Finger between my teeth, I closed my eyes and overrode the part of my brain that cared about self-preservation. The black tentacles wriggled upward, circling my torso, my chest, and my arm. This would be my only chance. I bit down hard. My front teeth cracked when they hit bone, but I muscled through the pain and kept clamping down, shaking my head like a wolf snapping a rabbit's neck. Jets of blood squirted into my nostrils and down my chin. Tendons squelched and popped. I howled through gritted, splintered teeth to cover the sound. Just as the tentacles reached my wrist, there was one final pop like a rubber band snapping. My middle finger fell to the floor. The shadow shriveled, loosened its grip, and shrunk to the size of a worm. Jerking deathlike toward my finger, it wrapped around the small sacrifice and burst into flames. It burned a blindingly bright green, then extinguished in an instant, cauterizing the finger's X-shaped wound.

The shadow was gone, but Milo was still there, huddled in a corner and gaping at me. I held his gaze for a moment before collapsing.

The next thing I remember was waking up in the hospital alone.

MILO AND I BOTH SURVIVED, but our friendship and my love for him didn't. No surprise there.

I ran into Milo again at a black metal show a year later. Seeing him across the bar sent a wave of panic through me, and I Googled the bands playing that night to make sure they weren't Nazis. No red flags popped up in my research, so I stayed, albeit far away from Milo. We stood on opposite sides of the room for the first band's set. It felt so different from when we used to crowd the stage, side by side, and throw up horns for every song. Alone, we sipped our beers and pretended to ignore each other.

I contemplated leaving after the first band, but Milo approached before I could sneak away. His shoulders were hunched. His eye contact faltered. I'd never seen him so awkward, and it gave me a strange sort of comfort.

"Hey," he said.

I chugged the last of my beer, preparing my exit. Just as I turned around, he grabbed my arm, but his touch was light, almost gentle. I waited for him to speak.

"I want you to know that I don't fuck with those guys anymore," he said. "The ones who are still alive, I mean. Don't fuck with their politics either."

I nodded for a long moment before saying anything. "Cool, man."

"Can I..." He scratched his neck. "Can I buy you a drink?"

My cheeks flushed. Since the last time I saw him, Milo had grown a beard and styled his blonde hair into a back bun. He looked cute. But I couldn't get sucked in again. Not after everything.

"Listen," I said. "If what you're saying is true, I'm proud of you, but, uh ... no. You understand, right?"

He nodded a little too long, then cleared his throat.

"Yeah," he said. "I get it. Well, uh ... I'll be seeing you."

"Right," I replied. "Have a nice life."

"You, too."

That was the last time we spoke. I still think about that conversation from time to time, and I hope he wasn't bullshitting me. I hope, for his sake and everyone's, that people really can change.

CAPTURE THE FLAG
BY DONYAE COLES

Skin. She wasn't called Skin then but that's her name and anyway it's not important what she was called then. She's always been Skin, always will be Skin, and Skin saw her first monster when she was eight years old. Heard the not-children singing for the first time then too, but it was the monster that made the impression.

They were at the edges of the playground, the not-children. Waving their flags and singing. She didn't know they were not-children then. Too far for her to see clearly, to catch the words she thought then but knows now weren't anything that her human ears could catch. What those things were, weren't anything that human eyes could really see. Her brain wasn't *low* enough to reach them. But it was on the level to see the monsters and that was level enough.

There was nothing special about the playground, but maybe her mom should have been more careful. Maybe she wasn't paying enough attention from the door, but past is past and it is what it is. The playground was one of those old, run-down half-cement, half-assed mulch thrown on the ground where a kid could fall from one of the rusting toys operations. On a hot day the silver slide would turn into a baking sheet but the wind was cool and fresh with a hint of winter on it, full of wet that would become a storm later.

Skin had seen the flag before. It was common, everywhere. She didn't think of it. Didn't think of the clear ring of the chain holders against the metal pole, providing harmony for those distant singers. She was there to play. Skin was a *child*. Her mother should have paid more attention, but the flags were really everywhere and this was not her mother's fault.

Not the American one but that other one.

It was the same colors but that doesn't mean anything because most flags are the same colors. Red, white, and blue. Flag makers really like that combination. Change the lines, the order, the percentages but still those three colors. So maybe the colors were part of it, maybe all the flags of the world had the potential to do what this one did if the wind hit them right, but Skin hadn't seen it yet. Maybe she would have if she were somewhere else, was someone else, but she was an American. And she was eight then and kids don't know shit. They know a lot but they don't know shit. They learn fast though and anyway, her mother should have paid better attention.

Her mother was having a smoke at the edge of the playground, opposite from those not-children, away from the other moms on the benches. She needed some time for herself, and that's not her fault. The world is hard, harder when you can see it, but maybe if she had paid more attention, picked a different playground, then it would have been a little longer before Skin saw it.

Skin wanted to ride the animals. Those sad metal beasts mounted on coiled steel beams. Skin thought it over carefully. There were three. A green lizard creature, possibly a dragon but not really magical enough to wear the title. A blue one that was supposed to be a bird, she was sure, but the wings were too stunted to ever fly. The orange one was the brightest. Closest to a horse, to the thing it was supposed to be. It called her and halfway across the concrete she'd already overlaid it with the animal she imagined.

The metal of the beast's hide was cool under her little fingers. She hoisted herself onto it, wrapped her hands over the rubbed silver handles attached to its head, just under the ears that were not quite right for a horse but close enough.

She rocked hard, the wind whipped past, lifted her braids, her unzipped coat. Her laughter came from her lips, pure and bright. *Skin was a child.* For one perfect moment she was everything she had dreamed under the cloudy sky. Skin the hero rode her mighty steed to great adventure and noble battles.

The boy met her downward rock with his hands. Pushed her so hard she went flying and landed on the thin mulch, scraped her palms on the concrete underneath. She looked up, her accusations dying on her tongue because it was a boy but it wasn't really. She didn't know what he looked like before, but she knew there had to have been a before because he couldn't have always looked like this. She would have noticed, her mother would have noticed if there had been a boy that looked like him.

His skin had that speckled look to it, like when you've skinned your fleshy bits, your arm or your thigh, just enough so it rubs the brown off and reveals a pale, red spotted layer beneath. No blood but wet with some clear fluid. Not water, not sweat, but something thicker, something oozing. He looked raw, like skinned chicken left on the counter for too long.

His face screwed into a sneer. His lips, pulled tight and white, showing blocky teeth, too many, too big for any child's mouth. The smile kept going, spiraled past the corners of his red-rimmed eyes, eyes and mouth one long opening. The whites of them pink, bleeding into the iris, spilling color. He looked like he had the worst case of pink eye. So bad that you could catch it just standing next to him, just breathing the air that touched him.

The clouds were too bright. Gray-on-gray sky, there would be a storm later but now just clouds and Skin couldn't look at them, they seared her eyes. The thing that should have been a boy was too close and a ringing in her ears that didn't make sense for the distance she had fallen, from horse to ground, clanged louder and louder. *The flag,* she thought, naming the sound. She looked at the boy again and could see it, see the pink mist of the door spilling from his ears and mouth, infecting the air but the door was in him, had become him and let something through. Skin was eight. She didn't know shit but

she learned quick and didn't need to see more to know what
she saw.

He called her a name, a word she wasn't sure she had ever heard,
at least not like this. She knew what it was, what it meant. It felt like a
punch. Felt harder than his hands when he pushed her.

He was so close. The not-children sang louder and higher, their
pitch reaching so far Skin thought her eardrums would burst, her
blood would turn into mist and she'd be like the boy, all twisted and
wrong. He opened his mouth and spit on her. Thick, yellowish, it
landed on her forehead, dead center. Baptized her in hate and phlegm,
and Skin was Skin from that day on, bless her soul.

She smashed her fist into his twisted smile. Threw all fifty-five
pounds of herself behind it. Felt hard teeth, and a wet splash of heat.
She thought it was more spit but it came up red so she kept swinging.
Turned raw face purple-black, twisted the nose out of shape to match
the smile. Her mother pulled her off him while his mother screamed
and shouted. Skin didn't hear, a whirlwind of fist and feet. Her mother
pulled her away, cradled her under her breasts and apologized, this
wasn't like her, she was a good girl.

"What's gotten into you?" her mother asked, shaking and shaking
her. The air around her mother smelled of Newports, menthol and
heat.

Skin tore her eyes away from the monster, tears mixing with the
blood and snot. No one else seemed to see the smile on his face. No
one else seemed to have noticed there was anything wrong at all with
him. No one else saw the twisted way his face had moved, or the gash
of mouth and eyes. The raw flesh and the wrongness of him. Just her,
so she was the bad one, she was the one who needed to be punished.

"Look at me when I'm talking to you!" her mother cried and shook.

Skin forced her face to turn away from the boy, the monster,
focused on her mother. "He spit on me."

Her mother nodded, stood up, and took her hand. "You should
watch your little boy better," she shot back at the angry woman, the
boy's mother who couldn't see him for what he already was. Skin's
mother didn't wait for an answer. Didn't have to see to know. Didn't

need to hear more to know. She couldn't see the monster but had lived long enough to know one or at least the signs of a boy that would become one. She hustled them to the car.

They didn't talk about it and they never went back, but Skin remembered. She washed her forehead raw but it burned where he marked her. Where his spit touched her. There was nothing there but she felt it. Never stopped feeling it.

It wasn't the last time she saw a monster. They flashed by her in the hallways of her high school, girls hanging on their arms. Saw them gathered at lockers, in the malls. Pink fog spilling from ears, wet, raw flash propped up on their twisted smiles. And everywhere, just in the distance, she could see the not-children, waving flags like the one that had waved over the playground all those years ago but different. Close but not quite right.

She didn't talk about it, didn't have to because then she started seeing them, the monsters, on the news. Showing up on reports like "eight dead in church fire" or "brutal attack on local immigrant community." No one else could see the monsters, but they knew. They didn't need to see what she saw to know. And everywhere, in those borrowed Facebook images and video confessions was the flag. Not the American one, that other one. Hung on walls, waving in the back-ground, on shirts, on cars, everywhere.

Monsters. Summoned from somewhere else. By design or by acci-dent she wasn't sure. It wasn't what they said though, that it was heritage or history. It was power that made them raise those flags, and maybe they knew what kind of nasty, twisted power they were getting with it, but Skin wasn't sure and she didn't care.

Over two decades later and Skin stood across a too-thin strip of grass while some Nazi shitheads screamed and swung a flag. Not *the* flag but another one that meant the same thing. And maybe it did the same thing when it was allowed to hang on polls and flap in the wind. In the distance she could see the not-children, hear their song. Above them the rings holding the flag, the one that summoned the monsters here, in America, sang in unison.

She thought about it as she watched the men who were not any longer men smile their too many teeth smiles. As the pink fog of the door spilled from them. As they spread their infection to anyone close enough to breathe it in. To anyone close enough to become like them.

She didn't understand a lot. She wasn't eight anymore and she still didn't know shit, but she knew enough. Knew that if the flag still whipped in the wind, then there would always be more. She didn't know if the flag called the not-children and they called down whatever made monsters or if it all went the other way round, the monstrous thing was already there and the flags, the not-children, just woke it up. Didn't know why they came as not-children and something else. Skin didn't even know why they were here at all. Did they feed from all that pain they caused? Was hate a physical thing at the doorway they opened? Did they swim in it, a pink pool somewhere in the gray matter of all those white boys she'd seen on TV. Of that white boy who spit on her? Didn't matter. She knew how to make it stop.

Had to make it stop because those things had come hundreds deep and sure they had matched the numbers on her side but Skin could feel it in the air. See the pink haze across the grass, see it spilling from some of the cops' helmets. It was so thick that even the people who couldn't see knew something was wrong. They danced from foot to foot next to Skin, twisted the poles on their handmade signs. The sun was out, bright and hot, but there was still a storm coming. They pranced like horses, ready for it.

And the not-children sang. They sang so loud, there were so many of them, swinging their flags at the edges of her vision. Like little patriots. *Like heralds,* she realized, the word spilling into her mind as she pushed through the crowd to see those raw-skinned things across the thin strip of grass.

Could have been that day in the playground all over again. Spiral smiles, cubes of teeth, rows of them grinding and snarling. They were talking, shouting, chanting really but she understood their words, the words of man. They spoke of genocide and rights and the way of life they were losing to people like her.

Her forehead burned and they sniffed the air, shifted, focused.

She wished she had a weapon, that it was true that the protestors, the rioters—the ones they label bad because they don't want to be eaten—carried weapons, but she didn't. She wished she had a bat to smash their overcrowded teeth down their fucking throats. She wished she had a brick. But all she had were her fists and feet. Same thing she had at eight. Same thing she would have, hopefully, when they lowered her into the ground.

"Fuck it," she mumbled and moved. She crossed the strip of grass. The cops noticed but moved too slowly. Skin wondered if she should have done this earlier but maybe they would have just eaten her earlier then. Her forehead burned. Maybe she was always going to end up there. It didn't matter. She was doing it now.

His tongue, as pink as his eyes rolled from behind his too many teeth to lick his pulled tight lips. He was sure, so sure that she would lay down and be eaten. Behind him, through the crowd, she could see the not-children, hear their song. *Heralds for the beast,* she thought.

The monster held a flag. The right flag, one of hundreds in the crowd. Enough of them to hold space, to hold it open for whatever was coming. A lot of flags and a lot of bodies that could become monsters, would become monsters. A lot of not-children. Their song filled the air and Skin didn't have to understand it to know what it was about.

No thoughts, just movement. Skin reached up, snatched the fabric and yanked. The monster, surprised, as surprised as the boy had been when she was eight, tumbled forward. The pole slipped from his hands, the flag clattered to the ground, its perfect position ruined. The heralds hissed and screamed. The crowd stopped, held its breath.

Skin spit on the flag. Gave the monster the finger. Leading by example.

Then it was all fists and feet and blood because the only way to defeat a monster, Skin learned that day when she was eight, was to make it swallow its own fucking teeth.

CONTENT WARNINGS

- Gordon B. White's "One of the Good Ones; or, It's A Gas": police violence, abduction, restraint, torture, tear/nerve gas, graphic injuries, homophobia
- Keith Rosson's "The Book of Veils": decapitation, dismemberment, homophobia, white supremacy
- M. Lopes da Silva's "Hostile Architecture": homelessness, hallucinations, gun violence, physical assault
- Cynthia Gómez's "Red Brick": description of violence by law enforcement, racist language
- Max D. Stanton's "The Four Magi of Motakwa County": racism, lynching, white supremacy, slavery, gore
- Patrick Barb's "The Pig-Men's Mud Motel": animal abuse, gore, drug use, kidnapping, racism, police brutality, suicide
- Ana E. Robic's "The Chad Show": self-harm, gore, dehumanization
- Caias Ward's "Snorting Ghosts in the Cause of Anti-Fascism": body horror, torture
- Sarah Peploe's "Beak": domestic violence, drug use, racism, islamophobia, transphobia, homophobia
- Sam Richard's "Blood & Honor": racialized violence and murder,

discussions of racism and homophobia, visceral depictions of self-harm and mutilation, implied domestic abuse

- John Baltisberger's "Box of Teeth": gore, torture, racism
- Jonathan Duckworth's "Lutznau's Opus": gore, incest, implications of sexual abuse, Nazism, direct references to the Holocaust
- Joe Koch's "Bride of the White Rat": animal abuse, domestic violence, transphobia
- J.V. Gachs's "Ay, Carmela": death, violence against children
- Eric Raglin's "'Til the Sun Wheel Turns No More": self-harm, homophobia, white supremacy, amphetamine use
- Donyae Coles' "Capture the Flag": racism, violence, body horror

Gordon B. White is the author of the horror/weird fiction collection *As Summer's Mask Slips and Other Disruptions*, and the novellas *Rookfield* and *In Her Smile, the World* (with Rebecca J. Allred, Feb. 2022). A graduate of the Clarion West Writers Workshop, Gordon's stories have appeared in dozens of venues, including *Nightmare, Pseudopod, The Best Horror of the Year Vol. 12,* and the Bram Stoker Award® winning anthology *Borderlands 6*. He regularly contributes reviews and interviews to outlets including *Nightmare, Lightspeed,* and *The Outer Dark* podcast. You can find him online at www.gordonbwhite.com or on Twitter @GordonBWhite.

Keith Rosson is the author of the novels *Smoke City, Road Seven,* and *The Mercy of the Tide,* as well as the story collection, *Folk Songs for Trauma Surgeons*. His short stories have appeared in *Southwest Review, PANK, Cream City Review, Outlook Springs, Phantom Drift,* and others. He is also a legally blind illustrator and graphic designer–which certainly provides its own unique challenges and rewards–with clients that include Green Day, Against Me!, and Warner Bros. More info is available at keithrosson.com.

M. Lopes da Silva (she/they) is a non-binary and bisexual author, artist, poet and soap maker from Los Angeles. They write queer California horror and everything else. Their horror fiction has been published or is forthcoming from *In Somnio: A Collection of Modern Gothic Horror Fiction, Neon Horror: Queer Horror Anthology,* and *Nightscript Vol. IV* and *V. Unnerving Magazine* recently published their novella

Hooker: a pro-queer, pro-sex work, feminist retrowave pulp thriller about a bisexual sex worker hunting a serial killer in 1980s Los Angeles using hooks as her weapons of choice.

Cynthia Gómez is a writer and researcher living in Oakland. She writes horror and speculative fiction and has a particular love for themes of revenge, retribution, and resistance to oppression. She has stories in *The Acentos Review* and *Strange Horizons*. You can find her on Twitter at @cynthiasaysboo.

Max D. Stanton is a bookish, morbid Dungeons & Dragons nerd who lives in Philadelphia with his common law wife and their two savage, unruly hounds. An unexpected meeting with the Devil inspired Max to take up a writing career. His first short story collection, *A Season of Loathsome Miracles*, is available from Trepidatio Publishing.

Patrick Barb is a freelance writer from the southern United States, currently living (and trying not to freeze to death) in Saint Paul, Minnesota. His writing appears in *Humans are the Problem*, *Tales to Terrify*, and *Boneyard Soup Magazine*, among other publications. He is an Active member of the Horror Writers Association. Fore more of his work, visit patrickbarb.com or follow him at twitter.com/pbarb.

A pseudonym since birth, **Ana E. Robic** is an antifascist artist and writer committed to chaos, abjection, and goo. Ana E. Robic enjoys a rich inner and outer life, and is religiously devoted to dissolving the border between the two—and indeed all borders. Previous works include the noise records *Powercize*, *How to Corner the Antique Doll Market*, and *Cephalopod, Undefiled*.

Caias Ward is a thick-wristed HVAC technician with over two dozen publication credits. A member of SFWA and Codex Writers, he currently lives with his wife and daughter in New Jersey, where he enjoys terrible movies and agitating for labor.

Sarah Peploe's short stories have appeared in various anthologies including Snowbooks' *Game Over*, Martian Migraine's *CHTHONIC*, and Three Drops Press's *A Face in the Mirror, A Hook on the Door*. She also writes and draws comics as part of Mindstain Comics co-operative. She lives in York and tweets @SarahPeploe

Sam Richard is the author of *Sabbath of the Fox-Devils* and the Wonderland Award-Winning Collection *To Wallow in Ash & Other Sorrows*. As the owner of Weirdpunk Books, he has edited and co-edited several anthologies, including the Splatterpunk Award-Nominated *The New Flesh: A Literary Tribute to David Cronenberg, Zombie Punks Fuck Off*, and *Beautiful/Grotesque*. Widowed in 2017, he slowly rots in Minneapolis.

John Baltisberger is an author of speculative and genre fiction that often focuses on Jewish Elements. Through his writing, he has explored themes of mysticism, faith, sin, and personal responsibility. Though mostly known for his bizarre blend of Jewish mysticism and splatter, John defies being labeled under any one genre. His work has spanned extreme horror, urban fantasy, science fiction, cosmic horror, epic verse, and he has even written a guide for mindful meditation. John has become known for his work in verse, having worked in both extremely short works and massive novella-length poetic epics. He continues to work to push himself to explore new avenues of expression and horror literature. He lives in Austin, TX with his wife and his daughter, and you can find more of his work at www.kaijupoet.com

Jonathan Louis Duckworth is a completely normal, entirely human person with the right number of heads and everything. He grew up in Florida and Germany, is a U.S.-Belgian dual citizen, and received his MFA from Florida International University. His speculative fiction work appears or is forthcoming in *Pseudopod, Beneath Ceaseless Skies, Southwest Review, Tales to Terrify, Flash Fiction Online*, and elsewhere. He is currently a PhD student at University of North Texas and an active HWA member.

Joe Koch writes literary horror and surrealist trash. Joe is a Shirley Jackson Award finalist and the author of *The Wingspan of Severed Hands*, *The Couvade*, and the forthcoming collection *Convulsive* from Apocalypse Party Press. Their short fiction appears in *Year's Best Hardcore Horror*, *The Big Book of Blasphemy*, *Not All Monsters*, and others. Find Joe online at horrorsong.blog and on Twitter @horrorsong.

J.V. Gachs is a Spanish classicist, writer, and aspiring librarian currently working as a Latin teacher. After many years without writing fiction, she got back to it during the Spanish pandemic lockdown in 2020. Since then her work has been featured in magazines such as *Luna Station Quarterly* or *Mordedor*, and Scott J. Moses' anthology *What One Wouldn't Do*. Obsessed with sudden death, ghosts, and female villains, she always writes with a cat (or two) in her lap.

Eric Raglin (he/him) is a Nebraskan speculative fiction writer, horror literature teacher, and podcaster for Cursed Morsels. He frequently writes about queer issues, the terrors of capitalism, and body horror. His debut short story collection is *NIGHTMARE YEARNINGS*. He is the editor of *ANTIFA SPLATTERPUNK*. Find him at ericraglin.com or on Twitter @ericraglin1992.

Donyae Coles is a horror and weird fiction writer. Her shorts have been published online and in anthologies. Her debut novel is a Gothic horror to be published by Amistad. You can follow her on Twitter @okokno and find more of her work at www.donyaecoles.com.